# THE SPIDER IN MY SINK

# THE SPIDER IN MY SINK

## A Journey Through Life, Love and Childhood

by

A. Marie B.

Published 1999 by

ORPHYN ANNIE PUBLISHING
P.O. Box 5261
Bellingham, WA 98227-5261
360-733-5543
www.orphynanniepublishing.com

Cover art and
Spider illustrations
by
C. E. Reasoner

Printed in the
United States of America

Third Edition

ISBN 0-9641427-0-8

0 1 2 3 4 5 6 7 8 9

FOR TIFFANY:
The greatest Spider In My Sink !

# ACKNOWLEDGMENTS

A deep and loving appreciation goes to my best friend and daughter, Tiffany Ann Loren Rowe. Without her love, assistance and years of understanding of what it has taken to create this book, I could not have done the work. She is simply amazing and truly the greatest spider in my sink. She and her husband, Benjamin David Rowe are the greatest inspiration for the beating of my heart. To my step-son, David Bangs, my other best friend, I express my gratitude for his support, friendship and assistance with the endless hours of computer work. He is immensely creative and he and his wife, Leigh are sincerely charitable people.

To Charles (C. E.) Reasoner, the delightfully talented artist who illustrated these works with the cover art and spider, I express my thanks. Because of friends like Jake and Kathy Lodato, Michael Otani, Martin and Frances MacKinnon, Gwen Boswell and her mother, Vernon Nash, members of the Holstrom, Anderson and Bangs families, and many other people who believe in me, my life is enriched in the purest sense. Friends and family are love, support and acceptance. Thank you everyone. I love you. May the true Medicine of the spider inhabit your lives and bring you peace and joy.

I am grateful to my spiritual guides who know me well enough to be the "inspiration" at just the right times by prodding, testing and sometimes gruffly guiding me. They have given me great strength and courage by blessing me with these writings. I know they are the force behind the work on these pages.

~ ~ ~

# A BEGINNING NOTE

Spiders are tenacious little creatures who cannot easily be discouraged from their life's purpose. As a child I sometimes sat in silent amazement, watching a spider build and rebuild its web through what seemed to be monumental adversities, like a gust of wind or a long stick occasionally interrupting its work. The wind was not my idea, but I did control the stick; not to be mean, but rather in childlike curiosity. I was testing the spider's determination by disconnecting a thread or two of its crystalline web to see what it would do. As it earnestly continued its delicate construction dance, that silly spider would not give up. Granted, spiders are creepy crawly things that tickle us in the night and send us into flailing frenzies trying to get rid of them, but you cannot ignore their sheer courage and fortitude!

In some American Indian legends and spiritual knowledge, the spider holds a place as the communicator of the first written language by weaving its mystical tales in its web. Spider, the communicator has become one of the earth creatures which has best instructed me on a pattern of life to imitate in the lesson of perseverance. Throughout my long years of life by trial and error, I have come to a simple comparison and decided we are all like spiders in a great sink, struggling against the odds of relentless challenges. I believe that people in every culture on earth have a common, delicate thread which links us all together - survival.

The Spider In My Sink is a kaleidoscope of the attitudes and emotions I have observed in some of these challenges in life and have written into the three chapters of this book. I have listened to the spiritual voice deep inside of me and I feel that I was given words to write down and share with you. There are writings in each chapter that are purposely simple and fun to read, especially with your children. In a few of the writings, I have taken license with the new use of "them" and "their" to denote a non-gender-specific reference instead of "he" or "she" so that both men and women can identify with these particular writings and see themselves in the words and thoughts.

It is my hope that you will all find a common thread in your life's experiences throughout the pages of this book. Some of these works reflect what I wish my childhood and life could have been like, or that I feel it should have been like. I have the same experiences, wishes and questions about life as many other people, and I certainly do not have all the answers. So, like you, I will keep searching and learning as I write my thoughts in poetry and prose.

When you are challenged in life with difficulties and frustrations, especially at times when you think you simply cannot deal with even the smallest of new or continuing problems, think of the spider's courage and don't give up! Wipe your teary nose on your arm, roll up your sleeves, and build and rebuild your life. Weave your adventures and lessons into a delicate, crystalline work of art, like the spider's web. If it gets torn down, rebuild it.

One of the most important issues we face today is the survival of nature. We cannot separate ourselves from the earth and the other creatures with which we share it. All life forms on earth depend on the same air, water and land to survive. Every form of life has a purpose, whether we humans feel we are directly served by it or not. We must help all of earth and its inhabitants survive through good politics, pure love and happy children.

The title of this book is taken from the poem, "The Spider In My Sink," which was written when my daughter was stricken with a rare and usually fatal bone marrow illness. We constantly searched for positive influences and experiences in order to keep her spirit connected to her body. We wrote the spider poem together to help us laugh and find strength for the new challenge we were facing.

In writing The Spider In My Sink, and sharing it with others, I ask you to consider living in harmony with the earth, maintaining genuine respect and support for all people of all ages (especially children), and celebrating your life in a positive way that will add to the peaceful harmony on earth. In my 48-plus years of adventures and observations, I have learned that life is a gift, the earth is fragile, and your soul is forever.

I am, in simplest terms, an instrument for expression. The words you read were given to me in inspiration. The knowledge and feelings belong to all of us.

A. Marie B.

~ ❖ ~

I say nothing that has not already been said.
I know nothing that has not always been,
is now, and always will be known.
There is no new knowledge,
only discovery of the soul,
and truth.

A. Marie B.

# TABLE OF CONTENTS

CHAPTER ONE:

A Journey Through Life — Page

# TABLE OF CONTENTS

CHAPTER TWO:

A Journey Through Love — Page

# TABLE OF CONTENTS

---

CHAPTER THREE:

A Journey Through Childhood Page

# Chapter One

## A JOURNEY THROUGH LIFE

There is a wonderful saying: "We are not human beings having a spiritual experience. We are spiritual beings having a human experience." As spiritual beings, we are charged with remembering our origins and our responsibility to the universal ordinance of harmony and respect. This is the guideline that tethers us to the great creator and the universe we call our home. Truth stirs deep within us, but is too often shrouded by our physical existence. The balance is to honor both the physical, and the spiritual truth with courage, humor and devotion toward all life forms on this magnificent earth.

## THE SPIDER IN MY SINK

The spider in my sink
reminds me of me.
It's tough and determined,
yet fragile as can be.
I flushed it down the drain
to drown it well, you see,
but each time I looked back,
it was looking up at me.
I spit on it with toothpaste.
I bubbled it with soap.
Then out of admiration,
I found a way to cope.
So now I spend my mornings
with a hero, I must think,
for I talk and carry on
with the spider in my sink.

**HANG IN THERE!**

## EXPERIENCE THE WHOLE

Feel the earth vibrate beneath you,
smell the air, know the scents
that tell of food or danger.

Taste the coolness of fresh moisture
on your tired tongue,
as you preen the dew from the leaves.

Let the heat from the sun warm your skin
through your thick covering
as the wind swirls around and cools you.

Know the quivering of your muscles
telling you when to run, when to leap,
or when to sit in silence.

Answer the call of kinship
with the vibrations in your throat
as you celebrate the news of others near.

Share the joy of real love, real friendship
in a lifelong romance with the same mate;
a union that bears wonderful offspring.

Live the respect and loyalty toward elders.
Follow the rules and know the code of ethics.
Keep the chain of survival strong.

Understand the laws of nature
governing all upon the great sphere
and know your place.

Accept death as you accept life,
knowing that each is the same;
to keep the balance.

Believe that the power you bring to earth
is the same power you take with you
when you leave.

Lift your face into the air.
Feel your heart beat as one with all,
keeping pace with the thread of life. . .

Be the wolf.

*We were made to be part of the animal kingdom*
*so we could learn to be more like God.*

~ ~ ~

# THE MYSTERY DANCE

Through
the mystic
spiral smoke,
into the soul
we glance. Hear the
words the ancients spoke
and see the spirits dance.
Watch the embers as they burn,
releasing scents to smell, teaching
lessons yet unlearned, casting the
ancient spell. A spell of love and caring
for life upon the earth; timeless wisdom
meant for sharing that follows us from birth.

~ ~ ~

## LIFE IS . . .

✦ Life is a series of perceptions interrupted by occasional realities!

✦ Life is made up of circles. Every circle that you participate in is complete. Across from someone who will not work, is someone who will. Across from the pessimist is the optimist. Across from someone who is uncaring, is someone who cares, and so on. Concentrate on the positive half!

✦ Life is the freedom to explore yourself,
to find out what lies deep inside of you,
to discover what makes you happy,
to decide what is best for you,
to learn how you are best at giving.
Life is the only thing you ever really own.

✦ Sometimes, life is like being rolled down a hill in a square barrel!

✦ Life has to have its ups and downs. Think of life as the blip on the screen of a heart machine. If it is showing a straight line, then you have stopped living.

✦

Life is peaks and valleys, so strap on your roller skates and go for it!

Life is timing!

~ ~ ~

~ ❖ ~

# MINKLE THE MONKEY

Deep in the jungle of Birra Moor, lived a monkey named Minkle. She was just like any other monkey in that she loved to swing from the Teekahko trees, eat delicious Marigola fruit and play all day. The problem was that she was very lazy and never liked to work. Instead, she spent all day bothering the other animals in the jungle.

Caprio, the leader of the monkeys, tried to tell Minkle that her laziness and teasing were going to get her into trouble some day.

"Minkle, you need to spend time working with the rest of the monkeys. It will teach you to get along with them and help you stay out of mischief," said Caprio. "And if you don't stop teasing others so much, you will be sorry."

"But, Caprio, this is so much fun," said Minkle. "I get to make fun of every creature in the jungle and it makes me happy to not work. That's all that matters to me."

Minkle never paid any attention to Caprio's warnings and she went on about her day. She simply did not care how the other animals felt. The Birra Moor jungle was filled with all kinds of creatures, so she could pester someone new every day.

One fine, warm day, Loumamba, the Lion was crouching under a Wickymicky tree, waiting for a Doogan's Deer to wander by. Minkle decided to imitate Loumamba and she laid on the ground to prepare for her own fake attack. Loumamba did not mind Minkle imitating him so long as she was quiet. Unfortunately, she started making pretend roaring noises and scared the deer.

"Now you have frightened my dinner away and I am very angry with you, you lazy monkey. Leave me or I will eat you instead," roared Loumamba.

Minkle could see that he was very angry and she ran into the jungle for safety. Loumamba again roared his disapproval and then turned and walked away.

After a while, Minkle came upon Wiebuck, the wild boar. Wiebuck was digging in the ground looking for her favorite roots and grubs to eat. Minkle imitated her and she made such a mess that Wiebuck could not see through the dust that filled the air. This made her very unhappy and she chased Minkle as she ran after her with her sharp tusks. The mischievous monkey managed to run faster than the boar and jumped up into a tall Teekahko tree to escape. Wiebuck grunted in disgust as she waddled away.

Just then Minkle noticed Jirgan the Giraffe eating his lunch of leaves high up in the Teekahko tree. Minkle scurried to climb out to the end of the branches. She picked the fresh green leaves and stuff them into her mouth before Jirgan could get to them.

"Stop eating my food you lazy monkey," scolded Jirgan. "I am very hungry today and you are picking the best leaves. I was eating here first and it would be polite of you not to eat my lunch."

The ruffled giraffe began to rub his head against the very branch Minkle was sitting on which made her lose her balance and she fell to the ground with a loud thud. The naughty monkey ran across the meadow as Jirgan laughed out loud and swayed his long neck back and forth.

Minkle rubbed her sore behind and then went in search of someone else to bother, or steal their food. It was not long before she came upon Pyntata the Python, quietly staring into the water of the beautiful Timbutu Pond.

"What are you looking at?" asked Minkle.

"Why, I am waiting for my dinner," Pyntata hissed right into Minkle's face.

Minkle was so busy mimicking the python that she did not notice it leering at her. She kept right on staring into the water thinking she was doing a great job of imitating the giant snake.

"It would seem my dinner has arrived," Pyntata hissed as she opened her mouth to swallow the foolish monkey.

Suddenly, Minkle realized the python was going to eat her and she jumped out of the way and ran for home as fast as she could.

*Knowing when it's time to work*
*or when it's time to play,*
*will help you learn to use your time*
*for good things every day.*

~ ~ ~

## HOMELESS

A tin can,
a dirty man
lying in the street.

A baby dies,
a mother cries
trying to make ends meet.

A cardboard cover
for friends who hover
with brittle, frozen toes.

A job lost
to save a cost,
and that's the way it goes.

Too many born
in countries torn,
give warnings we refuse to heed.

We can't stay alive
and help earth survive
while drowning in hunger and greed.

A tin can,
a dirty man
without shelter or food for the day.

A grey sky,
an old woman's cry,
the hunger just won't go away.

The rats near,
the dark fear
of life without a dream.

While others sleep,
a watch they keep
to hearken a harrowed scream.

A scream of hunger,
like roaring thunder
it beckons us to know,

that but for some luck,
we too could be stuck
in a life with nowhere to go.

~ ~ ~

## DEEP INSIDE THE WILLOW

Deep inside the willow,
weeps a tiny crystal light,
as the sounds of peace and silence
quiver sweetly in the night.
Through the wind that dances on the leaves,
speaks a voice so soft and clear,
to tell the earth how sad it is
the end is finally near.

And what to say of such a view,
has this whole time been a lie?
Did we know before we came to earth
we all had come to die?
You cannot take and never give
like an endless feasting knave,
for when the frenzy runs its course,
there'll be nothing left to save.

If we listen to the weeping voice
and know that what we do
can either make or break the earth,
each time that we pass through,
maybe a light of hope will shine
for all the world to see,
and earth and man can live in peace
through all eternity.

*Truth, like nature, will eventually*
*reclaim its territory.*

~ ~ ~

## *WE ARE*

*We are but one grain of sand,*
*yet we are the gentle beach.*
*We are but one fragile leaf,*
*yet we are the majestic forest.*
*We are but one drop of dew,*
*yet we are the churning ocean.*
*We are but one small pebble,*
*yet we are the deep river bed.*
*We are but one blade of grass,*
*yet we are the rolling prairie.*
*We are but one humble soul,*
*yet we are the whole of God.*

~ ~ ~

## OF WIT AND WISDOM?

It's just my opinion:

- *On Procrastination:*

Procrastination is a security device that assures us we will have something important to do tomorrow!

- *On Death:*

Being afraid of losing your soul to physical death is like thinking the sun will disappear if you cover your eyes.

- *On Survival:*

In the struggle for survival of the fittest, we must not forget the laws of give and take.

- *On Cooperation:*

We have exchanged compassionate cooperation for competitive consumerism. We must regaining our compassion.

- *On Leadership:*

When the position becomes more important than the responsibilities, you are no longer a leader, but a follower with ill placed power.

- *On Boredom:*

There is no excuse for boredom. It is self-inflicted.

- *On Obsession:*

Obsession in any form is the only real "sin." To be obsessed and dogmatic about any one aspect of life is like saying there is only one star in the sky.

~ ~ ~

# OF DARKENED DREAMS

Oh dreams of night and dark rapine,
of visions wrought with fear,
haunt me not, I long for veiling
from the truth you bring so near.

From puerility come the wolves of lore,
to tell of separation.
The pain it brought, not once, but more,
without thought of reparation.

So continued on like silken threads,
to weave a cloak of doom.
Each decade darker than the last,
cannot escape the gloom.

Of death and destruction I did see,
from adolescence until now,
foretelling of matters sure to be;
to each I humbly bow.

The faces of two men I saw,
one dead and one to die.
Three hours be past and so it was,
one died and one drew neigh.

"Years of death and sadness",
the voice called out to me.
And so it was from that day forth,
death surely came to be.

That my beloved was shown to me,
two souls of darkness came.
And thirteen days did pass to show,
they called my beloved's name.

Dreamed I a child I held in my arms,
begging for death to come,
to relieve the deep unbearable pain,
for life to be over and done.

Then to my child the illness came,
so great with death it fell,
to rest upon this blessed one,
to deliver her from hell.

Time passed and soon the proof was sure,
these dreams came once and more,
and twice the pain I felt of them,
as into my heart they tore.

Of floods and earth to open wide,
these dreams repeat each year.
Of famine and rage of human souls,
there is no end I fear.

Of buildings yet un-built to show,
the destruction of after the shake.
Of liquid fire and rain of black,
a hell on earth to make.

Of titanic armies and war machines,
through the valley of home they came.
Of endless night and blackened sun,
each hour to be the same.

Of broken byways and flames of death,
these dreams come one by one,
to warn of changes so severe,
that when the change is done,

This life on earth will never be
the way we live it now.
Comes the life of the fourth world,
unearthed by this evil plow.

Why can I not be nescient
of things before they are done,
so the pain I feel will not remove
what joy I have to come.

What good of knowledge of things to come,
when the news of them is bleak.
What possible reasons to know of these,
when of them I dare not speak.

And so to my dreams I yield each night,
by the hand of the Gods, it seems,
that I should know of things to come,
and be full of darkened dreams.

~ ~ ~

## RINKLE DINKLE DIAMOND BLUE

Rinkle Dinkle Diamond Blue
tried to learn to fly.
He fluttered, sputtered, flipped and flopped
as he tumbled 'round the sky.

His little tail just would not work
to keep his balance right.
He huffed and puffed and flapped his wings
from morning until night.

The starry nights reminded him
of sparkling fairy dew.
He closed his eyes to go to sleep
and in his dreams he flew.

He soared o'er hills and valleys.
He skirted fields of grain.
His tiny wings caught gusts of air
that carried him up again.

As the breeze washed o'er his face,
his little heart beat fast.
He never wanted this flight to end,
if only his dream could last!

Now Teeky Peeky, the magic elf
was watching Diamond's dream.
She wanted to help him learn to fly,
as simple as that seemed.

If she could keep him dreaming,
until the dawn drew near,
surely she could teach him to fly
by forgetting his trembling fear.

She needed to keep Diamond flying
just 'till he got the feel,
so that when he awoke out of the dream,
he'd be flying forever, for real.

So she reached into her magic pouch
and pulled out fairy dust.
She tossed it over Diamond's wings
and whispered, "Flying is trust."

"Trust in yourself, trust in your dreams
to keep them going strong.
Believe and try and never give up,
even when things go wrong."

Teeky coaxed and praised him,
until Diamond was flying himself.
He climbed so high and flew so well,
as he soared and waved to the elf.

He was so happy, he knew this was right,
because he would never let go
of the memory and incredible feeling
he now would forever know.

When Diamond Blue awoke from his dream,
he hopped to the end of the branches.
He kept in his mind that he had to try
and be willing to even take chances.

He threw out his chest, as it filled with air
and he spread his wings to fly.
He didn't give it a second thought,
as he caught the wind to the sky.

If you have a dream that you know is right,
and you want to make it come true,
then believe in yourself, give it a try
and your dreams will soon become you.

*There is never a soul more inspired to greatness than someone who knows that at least one other person believes in them.*

~ ~ ~

## THE MORTALITY OF FAME

How long can you hold your breath,
hold your soul so still,
balance so tightly,
tiptoe to the edge, or run.
Stay up, don't quiver, just deliver,
and don't try to blame
this flame,
just fame,
. . . sweet fame.

Smiles and kisses,
faces mirror the misses.
Set sights to straight lines,
aim high, act quickly,
eyes focused, soul steady.
Be ready, for it has no shame,
this flame,
just fame,
. . . sweet fame.

Friends come, friends go,
and love waits in the wings.
New places with new faces,
the adventures abound
to challenge the soul,
but never to tame,
this flame,
just fame,
. . . sweet fame.

Tracks fade and time plays a game
we cannot win.
Shadows dance on a last chance.
Take it, or fake it,
just don't let it go,
can't let it go lame,
this flame,
just fame,
. . . sweet fame.

Lights dim in a crowded room,
filled with memories and agonies.
The victories, like sand
on an ever-changing shore,
ebb and flow, come and go,
no more the same,
this flame,
just fame,
. . . sweet fame.

Another comes to steal the light
that shone but just for one.
It trickles down
a well worn crown
and soon the time has come,
to ease the hold on faded gold
and call this thing by name,
this flame,
sweet fame,
. . . just fame.

~ ~ ~

## THE THING YOU SEE

*The ground in*
*which it grows is*
*strong, its roots are*
*thick and deep. The*
*base of it is huge*
*and long, and up*
*its limbs do creep.*
*The covering is*
*coarse to feel, and*
*crooked are some*
*limbs. The aged*
*look it has*
*is real, its*
*shape comes*
*from within.*
*The deep and*
*noble scars*
*you see, are*
*from its grief*
*and strife. And*
*the more you look,*
*the better you see,*
*the thing you see is life.*

~ ~ ~

~ ❖ ~

## THE GARDEN OF EVE

During the time of the Garden of Eve, there lived many great and hegemonic Goddesses. They were wise, judicious and kind. There were many loving Gods in the garden as well, and everyone lived together in harmony and peace. Their garden reflected the nurturing nature of the Goddesses with the abundance of luscious greenery, fragrant, colorful flowers, gentle rains and a brilliant moon. The Gods' influence was evident in the warmth of the sun, magnificent moss covered boulders and powerfully rushing rivers which carved out the landscape throughout the garden. Everything and everyone worked together in rhythmic harmony, and the Garden of Eve was good.

The elder of the Goddesses was Leguz. She was powerful, caring, soft, round, feminine in every natural way, and the bearer of life to many new and wonderfully spiritual souls. The elder of the Gods was Tiwaz who was stalwart, intense, loving and the father of these new ethereal beings. Everyone knew and understood their roles and the importance of them in supporting each other and all life in the garden.

There were very few disputes, but if any arose, justice was quick and fair in manner. If there came a conflict between two beings, they brought it before the high council and whatever was decided became the method by which the dispute was reconciled. This was accepted and adhered to by all.

Leguz and Tiwaz had two sons. The eldest son, Hegelaz, was a jealous and selfish god who looked upon his parents' power as a barrier to what he felt to be his own right as the leader. This simply was his nature by birth and he had always shown a penchant for being irascible and impatient. He did not agree with the fact that the Goddesses were the ones who were the universal leaders. He felt that since they were generally smaller and obviously physically weaker than the Gods, it was simply illogical for them to be in such a prestigious position. He had felt this way since he was a small boy.

Now that he was older and had grown into his full stature as an adult God, Hegelaz's feelings intensified. He was tired of being in charge of only the rocks and rivers. He also did not want to simply have control over the thunder and lightening, but wanted to be the one who decided when the sun and wind would join in the symphony of the weather that played throughout each season, bringing life and death to the Garden of Eve.

The younger son, Jera, was a loving and brilliantly creative being. He was large and strong in stature just like Hegelaz, but his nature from birth was to be nurturing and kind. Hegelaz persecuted Jera relentlessly for this gentle nature he possessed, for it seemed to endear him to the Goddesses more than his own abrasive personality. This served as further proof to Hegelaz that the Goddesses were not fit to rule because they favored someone he considered to be weak and not a God of power and physical strength like himself.

There were a few other Gods who felt the same as Hegelaz, but they were not as vocal about their feelings. Hegelaz became the leader of this assemblage of discontented beings. Now, instead of taking their grievances before the council as they had always done, these insurgents of the Garden of Eve took to their own consorts and did not seek the balance of power of the high council. Many days and weeks were spent in disgruntled gatherings as these angry Gods became increasingly enraged with what they considered to be their unfair status. Plots to overthrow the Goddesses became the obsession of this band of malcontents and they dedicated their lives to the planning and enactment of such a deed. After many months of deceitful deliberations, a plot was born and agreed upon.

When it was The Time of The New Moon and all the Goddesses retreated into their Moon Lodge for the week-long ceremony, Hegelaz would make his move. The Goddesses were always their most vulnerable during this time each month and it would be easy to prey upon them. It was decided that while the they were inside their lodge, a great fire would be set all around the outside so that no one could escape from inside. Just to make sure Leguz did not live through this carnage, a deadly poison was added to the ceremonial incense she burned during her special prayers for strength and love.

Jera became aware of this insidious plot and wasted no time in telling Leguz and Tiwaz of what was to come. Tiwaz refused to believe that his own son could plot such an evil deed and he stormed out of the room where Leguz and Jera remained. Leguz tried to comfort Jera with the wisdom that no one need fear death.

"Death is simply a doorway to a new beginning," she told her grieving son. "When we Goddesses are in our lodge, during our ceremony we will pray for Hegelaz and all who share his anger. We will pray that in their quest for power they do not forget that true power resides in our ability to accept and live life in a way beneficial to the larger community supporting everyone. They must learn that when we are at peace in ourselves, peace flows from us. It does no good to impose our personal needs on others, for no one is the same and eventually, it will not work. Now go in peace and do not vex yourself over what is to come".

Reluctantly, weeping great tears of agony, Jera left his mother and returned to where the crowd of bemoaning Gods began to gather. As Hegelaz and his followers formed their clandestine circle around the lodge, they spoke with the other Gods passing by who would listen to their rueful rhetoric. Some listened, but others dismissed them as they went their own way, leaving Hegelaz and his band to their evil deed. Had they known what was to come, they would have taken steps to prevent what happened next.

The Goddesses were now gathering inside the Moon Lodge. When the last one arrived and found her place, the heavy door was closed. Leguz calmly spoke to them of the plot by the Gods to destroy them. She gave credence to the fact that some of them may wish to escape and were most welcome to leave. After all, some would need to live if the Garden was to continue to survive. Leaving was an act, Leguz promised, which no one would hold against them, It·was only right to let each one decide what her own future would be.

A few of the younger Goddesses gratefully decided to leave, and as they emerged from the lodge, Hegelaz asked them where they were going. They told him they had been advised to go home and tend to their lives in preparation for a new way of living which would last many millennia and would be difficult and strange to them. They were the ones who would bear the seeds of the future and must not perish with the others. Hegelaz was enraged at this revelation that the Goddesses knew of his plan. He hastened to complete his quest so that no more of them would escape.

Inside the lodge, Leguz lit her special incense and allowed the others to waft the deadly smoke over their faces so they could go to sleep and not bear the pain of physical death. Outside, the flames were ignited all around the wall. The fire grew in intensity, quickly engulfing the lodge and insuring the death of all inside. The remaining Goddesses who had escaped and the Gods who had not participated in this scheme, watched in horror and wept in agony at what they saw.

Suddenly, the Moon Lodge exploded in a powerful eruption. A blinding flash of light filled the sky over the Garden of Eve and lit up the night with brilliant colors, glimmering and sparkling as if all the stars and planets had exploded in ecstasy. A chorus of sweet feminine voices intertwined with the cascading rainbow of colors, glittering sparks, and smoky mist as it began to form miniature beings with opalescent, delicate wings. Everyone watched in awe as these tiny new souls flitted about, singing, floating on the warm currents of air, and tumbling about in the night sky like colorful little lanterns.

Through this act of greed and anger, the spirits of the Goddesses had been released to form new beings and new magic, more powerful and loving than ever. These new little souls were now the fairies of the kingdom, charged with reminding everyone to be gentle, happy and giving.

*By the fairies' light*
*and through the soul recall,*
*the way to love and caring*
*is the Goddess in us all.*

~ ~ ~

## DILLIDAWN THE DINOSAUR

Dillidawn the dinosaur
came back to life one day.
She wiggled, stretched and yawned,
as she wiped the sleep away.

Her eyelids fluttered heavily
as she peeked and looked about.
Her ears tickled, and she coughed a bit,
when she stuck her green tongue out.

As the light began to filter
through the opening of the cave,
she wanted to go out and see,
but she was not feeling brave.

She had not read a single book,
or even heard a song.
She had not spoken to, or seen
other creatures for so long.

What if they did not like her
or whispered when she was near?
She could hardly move a muscle
because of all her fear.

What if she said something dumb,
or fell down whenever she walked?
What if the whole world laughed,
or did not listen when she talked?

She spent so much time in fear,
that half the week went by,
before she got the courage up
to go out and just say hi.

Suddenly, a voice cried out,
"Hey Dilly, is that you?"
She froze in her steps, shook and cried
She was not sure what she should do.

"Please come out and join us,
we need another one,
to make our team complete,
and our work and play more fun."

Dillidawn could not believe
what the others had just said.
She had no need to fear them.
There was nothing here to dread.

Why, they were not even laughing,
and if some did, she did not care.
She would concentrate on all the fun
and good times they could share.

If you have just come back to life,
from times of fear and glum,
remember Dillidawn the dinosaur,
and if you are feeling dumb,

Hold your head up high, be proud.
You are doing the right thing.
Just by going in a forward step,
you will find the pleasure it can bring.

Like Dillidawn the dinosaur
who came back to life one day,
you and she will take the lead,
to help others on their way.

~ ~ ~

## FINAL FLIGHT

I fell into the air and found my wings.
I floated over meadows, hills and streams.

The earth I saw below brought tears of pain,
as I saw the fallen trees and acid rain.

Birds lay dying in meadows, trees and fields,
from eating poison greens; their deadly yields.

Rivers had all turned a deathly brown,
and once proud lakes were simply dusty ground.

Fish had long been gone from oceans deep.
It was as if the sea and shore had gone to sleep.

Bubbling and fumes from murky pools,
spread gases far too strong and much too cruel.

Animals disappeared from everywhere.
There were none to roam the earth, or fill the air.

The pain of all this dream was weighing great,
as my soul could see what came of greed and hate.

Then, slowly one by one my feathers fell,
as I tumbled back to earth. . . to live in hell.

~ ~ ~

*There are sacred places on earth where the energy is in perfect vibration for communication with the life force in all of us. One such place is in Arizona. As I walked the grounds, I wept in anguish over the loss of this holy place to a hotel now covering its gentle earth.*

## THESE HALLOWED GROUNDS

The sacred boulders
hold the voices of the past,
they know, they know.
The whispers of secrets
flash through the air
like misty clouds,
swirling, churning,
spinning
into a chorus
of off-key tones.

The voices bounce and fly
and softly land,
only to take flight again
as the delicate whispers
carry the ancient knowledge
over timeless changes
and eras anew,
never to forget
the lessons.

These hallowed grounds,
now violated
by constructed intrusions,
still cry out loud
to those who will hear,
and haunt the dreams
of those
who will always
remember.

It is a spiritual place,
a place where the earth's
own energy
creates vibrations
of strength,
where souls congregate
without interference
of extraneous
sounds.

It is a place
where pure energy
melds together to become
one brilliant ignition
for a moment
of fused intensity,
to recharge the souls
of those who come
to walk with God
in silence
and respect.

Not knowing,
believing
or understanding this,
there are those who come
to take for themselves
in selfish insecurity
and not give in return,
like a well
never fed
by rain.

But, for the souls
who hold the secrets
at the center of their being,
they know
this is
an ignorant violation
of the Great Spirit's command:
to keep the places
most holy,
holy.

By not keeping
these places as sacred grounds
for knowledge
and a link with the Creator,
by not allowing the earth
to facilitate this ancient ritual,
we are losing our tether
to our origins, and closing
the heavy doors
to the secrets
of life.

Without understanding
the laws of nature,
without acknowledging
the whole,
each civilization
that becomes "independent"
from the earth
and each other,
learns the lessons
too late.

*These hallowed grounds*
*echo the lessons.*
*We have but to be still*
*and listen.*

~ ~ ~

## BITCH BITCH BITCH

Bitch, bitch, bitch,
it's good for the soul.
It helps you get the hurt out
and even reach your goal.

If you don't release it,
it can bind your heart and hands.
Just remember not to let it,
be the last step in your plans.

It's good to see the faults
in problems you must solve,
but try to make the positive
your problem's last resolve.

And when your bitching's over,
you can breath a great big sigh,
for now you see the questions,
the what, the who, the why.

Now that you know the secret
to solving problems with a hitch,
make a positive plan to end with
and then BITCH, BITCH, BITCH !

~ ~ ~

## SO MUCH TO LEARN

We strive to be like everyone else,
yet we are celebrated and imitated
when we are not.
We live for acceptance from others,
but we fight for the right
to have our own opinions.

We always want what others have
and we do not see what is already
in our hands.
We remember the freedom of our
spiritual being, but we cling
to the senses of the physical.

We are born perfect, with the seeds
of the universe firmly planted
in our minds,
But we are taught that we are ignorant
of this knowledge and we must
ignore and forget it.

We pray to a God who "loves everyone
and of whom we are created
in the same image",
Yet we are taught that we are "evil,
born in sin and unworthy"
of that love.

We procreate in order to be fulfilled,
yet we abuse and blame our
children for our unhappiness.
We interpret life for our own convenience
and we indulge to avoid
the consequences.

We strive to gain distance from,
and control of the earth
and nature,
Yet our very survival depends on our
ability to protect and live
in harmony with them.

We worship perfection in everything,
but we despise those whom we
perceive to be perfect.
We come to earth to learn from our
experiences, but we spend most of
our time avoiding the lessons.

We have so much to learn.

*We are given periods of life to live in, learn from and leave behind either a remnant or a bolt of cloth woven from the threads of our experience. The choice is ours.*

~ ~ ~

## WING DING THE THING KING

If piles of junk were silver and gold,
Wing Ding the Thing King
was wealthy and bold.

But, he was just a collector of stuff and junk
that he kept in his room,
under his bunk.

He never shared it or passed it down.
He said he must have it,
especially his "crown".

Each day he gathered a little bit more,
and I simply don't know
how he got through the door.

There was so much junk under his bed,
when it reached the ceiling
he bumped his head.

As he went higher, he broke through the roof
and I'll eat my hat
if that wasn't proof,

That he had enough junk for the rest of his days.
That pile could have fallen
as it swaggered and swayed.

Well, he finally went through the top of the house
and he got so high
he looked like a mouse.

Then a big truck backed up to the door
and I could see by the load
they were bringing him more!

They pushed and they shoved it into the pile,
with Wing Ding climbing
higher the while.

Then "Poof!" it all vanished in a flash of blue light
and Wing Ding the Thing King
was nowhere in sight.

No one has seen him to this very day.
He just disappeared
and floated away.

I can't understand why he needed so much.
He never once used
anything that he touched.

Wing Ding the Thing King is gone now you see,
but the lesson he lost
he taught you and me.

We could all disappear in a great blue flash,
overtaken by greed
and mountains of trash.

You don't really need all that stuff
and that junk.
It will only collect
under your bunk.

~ ~ ~

## IDENTITY

*If we search for identity long enough,*
*through lifetimes of gender and race,*
*will we finally unlock the mystery*
*of why we live at a destructive pace?*

Maybe if we could re-awaken the meaning of our other lifetimes, we could better understand each other. We would realize we have all experienced being each other at some point in the space of time known as the "History of Humanity." Every culture, every lifetime, has something to add to the whole. I do not naively ignore the fact that human existence is crowned with violence and injustices on all continents. I simply, and with hope acknowledge the moments of discovery which have laced human history with periods of enlightenment. Hopefully there will be more . . .

## . . . OTHER LIVES

*The Beginning:*

I miss my lifetime in ancient Africa: the birthplace of the human experience. The haunting sounds of mellow drums over gentle waves of air, beckoning me home to a lifetime when the earth was our perfume, the fruits of nature were our adornments, and the spiritual purity of knowledge was unstained by the empty commercialism of this lifetime I now inhabit. How sad it is that so many of us have chosen to give up life's greatest lessons – living in harmony with the earth and our souls – in order to be a part of the frenzy that is becoming the destruction of everything: *rather like escaping a rain shower by jumping into a lake.*

*The Re-Awakening:*

I miss my lifetime in the Egypt of the Pharaohs and Atlantis: the billowing smell of the heated sands teasing the nostrils with dreams and wonders of life beyond the physical realm. Ethereal beings coming to be our teachers. The magic of knowing how to harness the powers of the earth in tune with the powers of our souls. Why must this current lifetime be a blatant denial of, and competition with the sweet knowledge of remembering the truths and realities of our natural state – pure energy: *rather like denying the law of gravity as we dodge the falling apples.*

*The Enlightenment:*

I miss my lifetime in ancient Tibet: The pure simplicity of a crisp existence, the twanging chords of tingling gentleness piercing our souls, resonating truth and light. The sweetness of knowing the lessons we must learn, intertwined with the rigid firmness of discipline. Enlightened ones imparting the "Laws of The Universe" – the most enduring knowledge in all the lessons of the earth.

Why do we trade this ancient lesson of peace, harmony and respect for earth for "modern technology" and commercialism, at the expense of hard-earned simplicity: *rather like trading a sack of beans for a can of beans.*

*The Beginning of The End:*

I miss my lifetime as an American Indian during the era when humans and the earth were friends: The rush of the seasons passing over the land, crickets serenading each new dusk, the fruits of the earth prepared for each new season. The freedom of the soul involved with the care of the earth, knowing where the blessings came from, listening to the spirits entrusted with our learning and understanding of why we must not take life for granted.

How can we tolerate other human beings being held in quarantine, suffering degradation and genocide as we selfishly turn our backs and ignore, or deny how they got there in the first place: *rather like saying that others "make their own beds to lie in" as you run away with the sheets.*

*Can a world so far from yours really be as close as your own mind?*

~ ~ ~

# MY HIDE IS MY PRIDE

My hide is my pride.
It tells others who I am.
I like to show it off sometimes
to everyone I can.
A zebra has its pretty stripes,
and a leopard has its spots.
You can tell a cheetah from the rest
by its own set of polka dots.

A monkey has its fuzzy hair,
a lizard has tough skin.
Birds have many colored feathers
to tell them from their kin.
A turtle has a hardened shell
to make itself a home,
and keep it safe from harm each day,
everywhere it roams.

Snakes have skin that slithers
every time they move.
Deer have different shades of hair
that goes down to their hooves.
The armadillo has its armor
to hide from one and all.
The giraffe has spots along its neck
that makes it stand so tall.

Crabs have shells that help them crawl,
and slugs have slimy goo.
Dogs and cats have fluffy fur
just like rabbits do.
Whales have tons and tons of skin
that helps them swim each day.
Sharks have teeth and pointed fins
that warn to stay away.

Beetles all have different shells
in a rainbow of colors bright.
Many creatures have coverings
that hide them in the night.
Frogs have lumpy, bumpy skin
to keep them cold and wet.
Fish have fins and lots of scales
that help them swim, you bet.

Plants have many beautiful colors,
even water comes in every shade.
And rocks and soil and minerals
show off the way their made.
It's easy to see that all of earth
has beautiful tint and hue,
And the whole world is proud of its color,
just like me and you.

~ ~ ~

*Upon arriving home one evening after surviving the lethal labyrinth of the rush hour freeway with its crazed and frothing participants, and resigning myself to the abuse in line at the fast food outlet (I tried to be friendly and accidentally went over my allotted three minutes for "personal service"), I sat down to the newspaper and the evening newscast on television. Reflecting on the general attitude which seemed to decorate my day, I was "uninspired" to write:*

## LAMENT OF THE '80s

It's not nice to be polite,
you get in people's way.
You really make them crazy
with the silly things you say,
like "please" and "thank you"
and "how are you today."
It takes up too much time
and time is someone's pay.

Hurry up, get through the line
and do not try to speak.
Now, did you expect the plumber's work
to really fix that leak?
Who do you think you are
making demands on someone's week
by trying to get your money's worth?
You really are a freak!

Get yours while the getting's good
and don't ever look back.
People can tell if you're a drip
by the anger that you lack.
Never mind if your boss is wrong,
you're really off the track.
Take your lumps and be grateful
that you didn't get the sack.

Please don't tell me you don't know
just how to be a slime,
or how to grease your way through work
and cheat on all your time.
I fear you're just not "with it" now.
You're really out of line
if you can't lie and cheat and steal
and know just when to whine.

What's that you say, you don't hate cops,
or own a "mondo" gun?
What's wrong with you, are you blind,
are you the only one
to think the world is safe and sweet,
or even any fun?
You'd better change your attitude
or you will be undone.

Now, surely you can tell me
there's a race of folks you hate,
to blame your daily problems on
and cry "eliminate"!
And if you can't resolve it,
then divide and segregate.
The boiling point will overflow,
you won't have long to wait.

Why, even politicians know
that nice guys finish last.
And if you get caught stealing,
write a book about your past.
If you're lucky, you'll get away
before the die is cast.
To find the route to riches,
do your dirty deeds up fast.

"Do unto others and then cut out"
is the motto of the day.
And "anything to make a buck"
is the new survival way.
So, if you want the world to think
you're hip, then you must say
"It's not nice to be polite,
you get in people's way."

*If you don't like how someone acts,*
*then don't act like them.*

~ ~ ~

## THE ILLNESS OF THE IVORY TOWER

**When lines are drawn and lands are gone,**
**the food of the soul is hate.**
**When the rich get more and the poor get poorer,**
**the anger ceases to wait.**

**When hope is gaunt and spirits haunt**
**those without light of day,**
**money makes sorely thin gates**
**to keep the anger at bay.**

**The history of man since time began**
**is riddled with violence and greed.**
**In all of time, the saddest crime**
**is we refuse the warnings to heed.**

**There is not one race, who in their face**
**is without guilt of hurting their own.**
**They betrayed their brothers to the others**
**for power and guided thrones.**

**Of religion and rule that is too cruel**
**that robs the hungering hoards;**
**what is made of a holy crusade,**
**save more for ladies and lords?**

**In the quest for more, you close the door**
**to the one true treasury room.**
**To be a fool to the golden rule**
**you've created your own doom.**

**A scene more daring is the art of sharing,**
**for it guarantees our survival.**
**The time has come to act as one**
**on the eve of death's arrival.**

**When the message arrives in the gifted lives**
**of peaceful men and women,**
**we tolerate until we hate**
**and take the life that was given.**

**Out of fear of loss, the foolish toss**
**their lots into circles of power.**
**They reach their goals, but lose their souls**
**to the illness of the ivory tower.**

**Don't judge the skin to the soul within**
**to say what someone is worth,**
**Or the path we trod on the road to God;**
**these beliefs bestowed at birth.**

**It's not the race that makes the face,**
**but what we do with the power.**
**And over time we've heard the chime**
**of yet another eleventh hour.**

~ ~ ~

# AND BY THE WAY . . .

- My short life's experience with things that have too many rules, is that there are also too many people trying to enforce them.

- Sometimes our best intentions fall into the great abyss of avoidance.

- The only thing you can take with you when you die is your opinion!

- Excess does not denote success!

- Don't just change your mind, change your attitude.

- Acknowledging and respecting people of all cultures honors the individual uniqueness in ourselves.

- Forgive and forget are two words that do not belong together. In order to forget, you would have to become amnesiac. However, it is critical, even to your own survival, that you forgive.

- The farther we get from the earth, the farther we get from ourselves.

~ ~ ~

## DREAMS

Through the mist of life, it seems,
we're always chasing after dreams.
Catch a dream and hold it near,
protected, safe and crystal clear.

~ ~ ~

# Chapter Two

## A JOURNEY THROUGH LOVE

The truest form of our spirit is pure love. The powerful white light of love that emits from angels, saints and spiritual deities in all cultures are simply rays of light from the same source - the creator. As human beings, we experience love in many forms, on many levels and for different reasons. Sometimes it confuses us, hurts us or leaves us feeling empty, but the most important source of love is the white light that emits from each one of us. We are already filled with love from inside and we are the conduits for these rays of light. Learning to be a courageous and gentle emitter of this light can sometimes be the most difficult challenge we face, especially when our physical experience is one of pain and disappointment. We must keep trying.

## *THE CYCLE OF LOVE*

*We are born,*
*we grow,*
*we learn.*

*We meet someone,*
*we become friends,*
*we become friends and lovers,*
*we become friends, lovers and parents.*

*Our children are born,*
*they grow,*
*they learn,*
*they leave.*

*We become friends again,*
*we become friends and lovers again,*
*we become friends, lovers and grandparents.*

*Love has been as it should be.*

~ ~ ~

# REAL LOVE

If I open up my soul to you,
will you stand and watch me bleed,
or will one drop pass o'er your lips
and you'll understand my need?

Do you know yourself well enough
to see inside my mind?
Are you strong enough within your soul
to be gentle, soft and kind?

Are you sure you have a footing
on your image of your own,
or do you fear to let love in?
Do you want to be alone?

May I lean upon your shoulders,
if I ever feel the need,
and hide behind your stature
from a world of hate and greed?

Of all the people that I know,
I trust you most of all.
So, if I stumble on my way,
will you catch me when I fall?

Could you let me cry in agony
without falling all apart?
Would you let me share my fears,
and unburden my own heart?

Would you think me weak and ugly,
if I weren't always strong?
Does it turn you off to see someone
who doesn't always "get along?"

Do I have to be a perfect mate
for you to love me true,
or can I be just who I am,
and you can just be you?

And when my need to be afraid
lessens as time goes on,
I'll be right here, my love and friend
for you to lean upon.

~ ~ ~

## ABOVE ALL ELSE

**Up**
**higher**
**than the**
**highest ground,**
**above the granite**
**splendor, the loving**
**hearts of countless souls**
**give life so warm and tender.**
**Providing air for all who breath**
**and shade to others lives, hardened**
**by the flames of fire, this friend of**
**God survives. A home to some and food to**
**more, without a word it shares, asking little**
**from a world where so few truly care. With gentle**
**arms of luscious green and roots so deep and free,**
**grand in structure,**
**grace and form,**
**above all else,**
**stands the tree.**

~ ~ ~

## STRAIGHT FROM THE HEART

- God created love so that fear would have a pillow to rest its weary head upon.
- Simply because you have experienced a disappointment, does not mean you should become one.
- Being in love forever means two people, knowing it can end at any time, working together to make sure that it doesn't.
- Life is filled with risks and a few adventures. When you come to an adventure with a few risks, take it!
- The family is the foundation on which is built strength, hope, love and happiness.
- It is interesting to note that the letter "n" in both the words man and woman is shaped like the pillars of a doorway, supporting each other and the "structure" for which they are responsible as a team.
- Lifetimes come and go, knowledge feeds our soul, but love carries us through eternity.

~ ~ ~

## THE SUPPORTING ROLE

"I get so tired of just being the support,"
I hear some people say.
"If only I could play the lead role,
the part everyone wants to play."

"No one notices me behind the scenes.
I'm insignificant in what I do."
Well, I'm here to tell you all, my friends,
that statement is not true.

The most important part of all
is the support that's seldom seen.
There would be nothing else to notice
without something on which to lean.

Everything in life depends on something
for support and a helping hand.
If not for the columns in a single file,
the majestic temple could not stand.

Without support, a bridge would fall,
skyscrapers would tumble down.
The "Greatest Show On Earth" would be sad
without the humble clown.

If there is no support from parent's love,
a child will grow up sad,
without memories of a family life
and the good times they all had.

With nothing on which to hang or stand,
art would not exist.
The world would float into outer space,
if gravity did not resist.

Big Ben in London could not tell time
without the gears behind the face.
So you see, my friend, support comes first.
It serves in the most important place!

~ ~ ~

## REACHING OUT

Aching for common ground,
peaceful friendship,
        understanding life's lessons
        without simply trading obsessions.
                Inspiration without saturation,
searching for that "soul mate"
who already knows you
        inside and out,
        throughout time and space,
                enough to love you forever.
Wanting the spiritual,
hooked on the physical,
        blurred visions of what is to be,
        just letting love see
                what comes of life together.
Expecting too much,
always wanting to touch,
        needing constant validation.
        Not knowing when to give or take,
                the union comes to an end.
All that was needed
was the will to understand,
        to lend a hand
        as each one struggled,
                taking turns needing, giving,
                . . . it could have been forever.

*Love without friendship*
*is like a rose without a stem.*

~ ~ ~

## IN THE SHADOW OF A DREAM

In the shadow of a dream,
lies another road to travel,
though the way may seem
hidden by the gloom.

When a door that leads to hope
is locked and you are baffled,
look around and see the doors
to other rooms.

In the quiet of a letdown
you can hear another voice
say, "There's surely something else
that you could do."

If you listen, you will find
you have another choice.
Inside the stillness of your heart
could be a clue.

Sometimes while you are weeping
and shaking from the fear,
you think of how your life
should go your way.

Life doesn't always bring you answers
in the way you want to hear,
so you curse it
and you try to turn away.

It's all right to become angry,
it's all right to sit and cry,
for you need to let the fear
inside you out.

Just remember as you're searching
for all the reasons why,
the simple answers
are the ones you shouldn't doubt.

~ ~ ~

## THE RIVER OF LIFE

Over peaceful rivers flow sparkling drops of dreams, life, memories, hopes, fears and sorrows. Brought together by rushing time and forces unseen, the river runs deep, wide and powerful, carrying us to our future, giving us experiences of today and creating memories of what was. The subtle reeds, grasses and underbrush gently soften the shores, catch the wind in their flowing tresses and whisper to us to keep going, don't give up, even when the river is too rough and dangerous. There are twists and turns that will take us by surprise and cause us to lose our way, just for a moment. But the river is constant, giving us life, showing us the way. We have but to follow and trust.

~ ~ ~

## THE ARMADILLO'S PILLOW

The armadillo had a pillow
made with magic in its seams.
It brought happiness and love
to the armadillo's dreams.

The other animals would wonder
why she always had a smile.
They admired her persistence
and her cheerful, helpful style.

Each day the 'dillo wandered
through the forest 'round her home.
She scurried and she hurried
over stumps and clumps and stones.

If danger came too close,
she would roll into a ball.
Protected by her armor,
she could hide from one and all.

But her greatest way of dealing
with the troubles in her life,
was her positive persistence.
It got her through the strife.

Each evening, when the shadows fell
and it was time to go to bed,
the armadillo tucked the pillow
gently underneath her head.

As she dreamed, she learned the secrets
of making life a gift.
She simply let the good come in
to give herself a lift.

When she awakened in the morning
and remembered all she felt,
'dillo shared the good with all
and was always glad to help.

The other creatures in the forest
liked the goodness she had shown.
They wanted to be happy
and have pillows of their own.

The armadillo told the others
it was not so hard to do,
if you simply keep the goodness
flowing in and out of you.

So when you go to sleep at night,
keep goodness in your dreams
and you will have a pillow
made with magic in its seams.

~ ~ ~

## *I WISH TO BE*

*I do not wish to be*
*as the unyielding oak,*
*nor the leaning sapling,*
*which allows the wind*
*to blow it 'round.*
*Nor do I wish to be*
*as the rock that stands*
*cold and lonely*
*on a deserted beach,*
*to be visited only*
*by an occasional gull,*
*or splashed by a pounding,*
*chilling wave.*
*I do not wish to be*
*alone and forgotten,*
*tucked away*
*as last week's newspaper,*
*the vital stories*
*too soon replaced*
*by emotions of the moment,*
*thought of only when the floor*
*is washed, or the new puppy*
*is being trained for indoor living.*

*I do not wish to be*
*pitied or soothed,*
*usually ignored,*
*thought of only*
*when solicitations*
*are pushed through the mail,*
*or TV reminds*
*of needed love.*
*I wish to be a living,*
*constant part,*
*of a thought,*
*a part of a moment,*
*a part of a wish,*
*of someone who . . .*
*does not wish to be*
*as the unyielding oak,*
*nor the leaning sapling*
*which allows the wind*
*to blow it 'round.*

~ ~ ~

## NO PAIN

Don't want no pain in my life,
don't want no grief, no strife.
I don't know
how to make it so.

If I never fell in love again,
never had another friend,
I'd have no more sadness,
but no gladness.
I could cure the madness,
but I'd have less.

If a friend becomes a lover,
does the friendship have to end?
Why can't we be the same to each,
why do we just pretend?

If the answers to these questions
is always, "I don't know,"
how can we find the key to life,
an end to strife,
a man, a wife?

Could the secret be
inside of me,
maybe covered by the fear
of being near,
not knowing how to touch
and such?

Do we really have to be involved
with what's "happening and in,"
or can we lean on inner strength
to know just how to "win?"

Win at what
and who will know,
if we did or didn't give
in a romance,
if we took the chance
and lost the dance?

When we grow old
our face will show
the times we had before,
when we reflect
on friends and loves,
if we really needed more.

~ ~ ~

## ONE MOMENT PLEASE . . .

The hissing steam rises from the gently curving metal edges of its heated resting place, as the aroma of hearty flavors mixes with the fresh morning air and fills my tingling nostrils. Ahhhhh, this is comfort. This is happiness, security, and memories of delightful childhood moments. It is moments of laughter and togetherness, of peaceful, lazy mornings. This is a space in time where the angry world cannot reach me.

A small light flashes, signaling the time when the cause of these emotions will soon be the reason for my next feelings of happiness and contentment. Somehow, I know I am comfortable with others who pride themselves in the ability to experience realities such as this. I know they are good people, humans of like realities and dreams. My mouth salivates as I tenderly grasp this incredibly wonderful object, this home remedy for anxiety and stress. Its correct preparation is vital to the final effects of my utter and complete rehabilitation. After all, I am only able to do this ritual one morning per week. I have no time on any other day.

My mouth continues to water, my nostrils twitch, my lungs fill with the smells, and the flavors strike just the right areas of my tongue as I take the first bite. My body responds to my mental contentment and I know I have once again brought a healing moment into my life. This is my time, my space, my moment of solace and escape that I love so much. This is my waffle!

~ ~ ~

## THE SAGA OF HELEN SWEET

The aged ones, the ones who know
how times in life can turn,
are the ones we need to respect and heed
the lessons we must learn.

For without the old, the stories aren't told
and life repeats without purpose.
It is through their eyes we can become wise
and let the good in life surface.

We live in a day where we throw away
the very young and the old.
We cling to an age that is center stage
and our selfishness is quite bold.

Now, I'll tell you a story of a wise old one
who always lived life to her best.
She never cried foul, or talked with a scowl
and she lovingly cared for her "nest."

And over time, her only crime
was growing too old to stand,
or walk very fast, or talk of the past,
or lift her food with her hand.

When her funds ran low, she'd have to go
to a "home" that's not really a home.
She told all around, she'd have to be bound
to take her, so leave her alone.

She knew if she left her home and friends
she would not live much longer.
And sure as she spoke, her heart was broke,
for they knew she would not get stronger.

They took her away to the "home" to stay
and she died without dignity.
As her smile was taken, her will was shaken.
She simply let death come to be.

In the end, without a friend
to keep her dark world sunny,
this brave woman died without her pride,
simply because of money.

This story is about each of us
and how life goes 'round and 'round.
We are all silly fools if we think these rules
don't apply or exceptions are found.

In your old age, as you turn the page
to see if your life is complete,
just remember this story of life without glory
and the saga of Helen Sweet.

*We are the babies, we are the young,*
*we are the old.*
*We are the stories of life and the future*
*as yet untold.*

~ ~ ~

# THE PAIN OF LOSS AND DISAPPOINTMENT

How fancy we float
when the pain becomes too much
and we seek the sweet reprise
of a softly sung song.

The music brings a healing remedy
and smoothness
that cannot be found in speaking.

When words cannot repair,
music makes its mark
and sinks us into a sound
we can bear.

After the crying comes no more,
for the crying returns the pain,
we seek other ways
to comfort our aching heart.

We turn to talk, buying things,
traveling, new friends
and finally to the truth and God.

We learn that pain is part of growing,
part of learning to appreciate life.
For if life were too easy,
we would surely take it for granted,
as we do so many things around us.

We need not look for pain
to be a proven person,
but we must learn to accept
that which is not in our control,
the pain we cannot foresee.

What matters is how we handle
these extreme challenges,
how we become afterwards,
what we do with our life,
after we realize that what is, simply is.

This determines how
the rest of our life will be,
not just what happened to us,
but what we did about it.

So we begin to understand
we can appreciate and enjoy
the sweetness of a sadly sung song,
so long as we also listen
to the music of life,
be it sad or joyous.
For we are the violin,
and God is the bow.

*Every time a loved one dies, a new star is born in the sky and another guardian angel gets their wings.*

~ ~ ~

*How did we manage to trap ourselves into believing everything we read? Why has perfection replaced uniqueness? How did men and women ever accomplish falling in love before we had all the experts and publications telling us how to find:*

## THAT PERFECT MATE

I'm looking for that perfect mate,
the one they show you in the ads.
I want them to be mine, all mine,
to make me happy when I'm sad.

They cannot have a single flaw,
or annoying personality quirks.
I want my relationship to be honest,
the way the one in a magazine works.

I've read all about how to be "balanced,"
or know if your sweetheart is cheating.
I've read what to expect from a romance;
basically, everything that's worth reading.

I read in a book just what to say
if you know that someone is lying.
Then I saw an expert on TV
who said to just keep on trying.

We'll take one of those magazine tests,
to tell if someone is right,
and if they can't pass with a perfect score,
then they can only spend the night.

They must know themselves extremely well,
just like I know about myself.
And if their body is not perfect and young,
I'll know they do not care about health.

They can't be too ugly, unless they're rich
and they must wear all the right clothes.
They must know all about food and wine.
I won't be without someone who knows.

Their income must be high and solid,
because I will not live with a leech.
They must have a six figure income,
a one figure body, and perfect speech.

Someday I'll meet this perfect mate,
who has read the same things as I,
because the latest article said,
"In love, you must reach for the sky! "

I deserve it, oh yes, that perfect love,
because I've learned all I need to know.
I've passed all those tests myself, you see,
and I'm sure my "knowledge" will show.

So, the next time I go searching,
for someone perfect to fit the bill,
if they can't be totally perfect themselves,
well, at least I know I certainly will.

~ ~ ~

~ ❖ ~

## THE SEEDS OF CHARITY

In a field of beautifully decorated flowers lay an average looking young lady, enjoying the peace of the moment. A gentle breeze tickled the flower petals, causing them to dance about in patchwork swaths of brilliant colors. This was not just any field of flowers, however. These were magic flowers. Whenever the young maiden gave even one flower to people in the village, each one who received them instantly felt wonderful, happy, and healed from their pain and sadness. Everyone was grateful to her and showered her with praise and gratitude. This made the maiden feel needed and important.

The young lady's mother, a wise and gentle soul, worked very hard to keep the flowers planted, groomed, and growing for each harvest. She toiled day after day, hour after hour, carefully planting and grooming the seeds as they grew into their magnificent, special blossoms. She was happy to do this laborious work as she knew it would bring joy to so many people. Every morning, before the sun came up, she quietly donned her tattered robes, worn-out boots and ragged scarf to spend the day in the garden. She was careful not to wake her sleeping daughter who would rise later to begin her own chores of cleaning the house and preparing the meals.

Two years earlier, the mother happened upon a mysterious vendor at the village market who presented her with the seeds. The most important part of growing them, the vendor warned, was to make sure no one picked all of them at the same time so that enough seeds would be left to plant for the next harvest. If this rule was followed, the flowers would last forever.

The young lady discovered the magic of the flowers quite by accident when she gave a beautiful bouquet to a passing farmer and his gravely ill little boy. As soon as the maiden handed him the flowers, the small boy smiled and laughed and hugged her gleefully. He felt very good indeed. The farmer was so surprised and grateful for this, as it had been a long time since his son had been well or happy. The young lady felt wonderful for having done this good deed and her mother was pleased that she could now share this wondrous secret. From then on, whenever the girl saw someone who was ill or sad, she gave them a few of the blossoms. The warmth and love were always good to share.

People from far away began to hear about the mystical flowers and they too wanted to have some for themselves. Soon, more flowers were needed to give away and there came the danger of not having enough left to make the seeds with which to grow more. The daughter had become so obsessed with the adulation of the people who idolized her for her ability to give them these healing bouquets, that she lost her ability to reason the prudent stewardship of these incredible sources of joy.

The young woman became argumentative with her mother over how many plants were to be held in reserve for seeds and how many were to be given away. Having never participated in the tedious work of growing and tend them, the daughter could not fully appreciate why she could not pick all of them.

"How could I possibly tell people I have no flowers to give when they depend on me to make them feel good? This simply is not fair," she said.

The maiden could not deal with her fear that if she did not give them flowers every time they asked for them, people would stop thinking she was wonderful. It would be embarrassing and she would lose their affection and approval.

One day, a great crowd of people traveled many long miles and came to the flowering field. They pleaded with the young maiden to give them each at least one. She was hesitant at first and the people become more urgent in their pleas. Surely she could not be so insensitive as to refuse them just one flower. The maiden finally gave in to their request. As she began to pick the flowers and hand them to the grateful crowd, she once again became so absorbed in their praises, that she lost track of how many she had picked.

When the last person in the crowd walked away holding their magic blossom, they took the very last flower in the field with them. The young lady waved good-bye and then turned to look at the garden. When she realized what she had done, she sat down in the empty field to cry.

*When you simply give your charity*
*to make yourself look good,*
*you're not really thinking of others,*
*or giving the way you should.*

~ ~ ~

## A FRIEND IN DEED

"A friend in need is a friend in deed,"
or so the saying goes.
Can we get past the fear and greed
to find out just who knows,

how to be a friend and really love
another human being,
by accepting all the doubts and faults
that each of us keeps seeing?

It doesn't matter if we're perfect,
or always full of fun.
We still need each other, all of us,
we really all are one,

and one for all
is what we truly need,
to get us past this time of grief.
It's time to plant the seed;

the seed of love and caring
for other human souls,
to make the common good of all
a common set of goals,

for each to follow and teach again
to children being born.
We can learn that peace and love
will heal the gashes we have torn.

A hug, a smile, a thank you,
or a word to say you care,
will be returned tenfold
from the love you share.

So give a moment, a kind word,
or lend a helping hand
to those who need another soul
to help them make a stand.

As we reach out to others,
we enrich our own lives too,
for sharing love and kindness
will bring it back to you.

We can make a world of difference
from beginning to the end.
We can make the world more peaceful,
if we make a world of friends.

~ ~ ~

## WHEN FRIENDS LEAVE US

When friends leave us,
we think the world will end.
We think we will never feel
the same love and encouragement
that we shared with each other.

When friends leave us,
we think we cannot open our hearts
or trust another person.
We think we cannot give again
as deeply as we did before.

When friends leave us,
we think the world will forget us.
We think that life will go around us
and not remember that we are here.
We think we will simply disappear.

We are wrong.
The world knows no bounds,
has no ending, save the change of seasons,
even then to come again, not as before,
but new and unique.
So it is with friendship.

~ ~ ~

## *CARESS ME*

*Set your gentle touch upon my face.*
*Twist and twirl my tresses*
*in your grasp.*
*Know me well*
*by surrounding my body*
*in your strength and power.*
*Mix our scents*
*with your moving breath*
*and know that we are one*
*at this moment, and always.*
*Let me breath you*
*into my very soul*
*and feel your vibrations*
*through me.*
*I have known you*
*through all eternity*
*and my dreams float*
*upon your every move.*
*Caress me, oh gallant wind.*

~ ~ ~

## DON'T FEAR YOUR NEEDS

You are frightened, as am I,
but love is patient and time is there.
Peace comes slowly and happiness
is everlasting.
You are gentle and so full of love.
Don't fear your needs,
for when they are fulfilled, you are strong
and able to give of yourself.
Be only of yourself,
and you are all that you should be.

~ ~ ~

# NEVER EAT YOUR SNOWMAN

Give him eyes of rocks or coal,
a nose of carrot, a mouth so droll.
Place a pipe between his teeth,
give him a twig and holly wreath.

Smile at him and ask him to play.
Bring him a hat and a new red sleigh.
Let him dance and sing with you,
but there's one thing you should not do:

NEVER, NEVER, NEVER
EAT YOUR SNOWMAN !

If he needs a scarf around his neck,
give him one and what the heck,
give him a coat if he looks cold,
or a bright green tie, if you feel bold.

Umbrellas are handy in the snow.
Feed him snow balls to make him grow.
A new watch is what he could use,
and warm galoshes, or fuzzy shoes, but:

NEVER, NEVER, NEVER
EAT YOUR SNOWMAN !

If you want he to be a she,
just place a wig where it should be.
Give her jewelry and makeup too,
and a briefcase, now that should do.

Place a book gently under her arm,
and give her stockings to keep her warm.
She might use a cane, if she is old,
or a walking brace, so I'm told, but:

NEVER, NEVER, NEVER
EAT YOUR SNOWMAN !

Give her glasses to help her see,
or a bouquet of flowers, without the bee!
Put gloves on her hands made of twigs.
You can even teach her to do a jig.

Give her earmuffs to keep out the wind,
or an innertube to take a spin.
She'll need skis and very big poles
if she's to ski over hills and knolls, but:

NEVER, NEVER, NEVER
EAT YOUR SNOWMAN !

Invite your friends into your home,
so your snowman won't be alone.
Give them tea in a special cup,
let them see him all dressed up.

How about a Walkman to listen to tunes,
and if he's to eat, he'll need a spoon.
You could eat with him and always dine
on real ice cream. Won't that be fine, but:

NEVER, NEVER, NEVER
EAT YOUR SNOWMAN !

A big woolly blanket is a nice touch
to wrap your snowman up and such.
Or let him sleep in your bottom bunk,
if you can find him under all that junk.

When winter and the snow are gone,
and the ice is melted from the pond,
remember you'll have a friend next year.
So be glad you always held him dear
and . . . . .

NEVER, NEVER, NEVER
ATE YOUR SNOWMAN ! ! !

~ ~ ~

## *TRUST*

*If I could trust, I could live.*
*I could swallow life whole*
*and not choke.*

*If I could trust, I could give.*
*I could share love freely*
*and not hide.*

*If I could trust, I could feel.*
*I could live life openly*
*and not bleed.*

*If I could trust, I could laugh.*
*I could feel joy simply*
*and not retreat.*

*If I could trust, I could cry.*
*I could feel pain deeply*
*and not die.*

*If I could trust, I could breath.*
*I could share life and be happy.*

*If I could trust.*

~ ~ ~

~ ❖ ~

## THE QUEST

Under a majestic, moonlit sky sat an old warrior. Quietly staring into the heavens, he counted the stars and listened to the songs of crickets carried on the gentle night breeze as it whispered secrets of life. Suddenly, a star in the center of the sky began to sparkle with increasing energy and grew into a blinding ball of light suspended directly in front of the warrior. He shielded his face with his forearm as he turned his head away from the glare. From somewhere inside the intense light, a deep, comforting voice spoke to the warrior.

"Because you are strong and live by your heart, you have been chosen to complete a dangerous and vital quest. It is the most important task you will ever fulfill. Do you wish to do this?" the light questioned the warrior.

"What is it that you want me to do?" he asked bravely.

"I cannot tell you until you have decided that you have the will to do it," replied the voice.

"How can I know I have the will if I do not know what you ask of me?" catechized the warrior.

The glowing light gave a quiet, yet firm answer, "It is simple. Either you have the will, or you do not."

Meeting the challenge, the man stated honestly, "I am the most bold warrior in our village and I have braved many difficult things. I have the will to be strong, this I know."

"Then you will do it?" the voice of the star

asked once more.

"Yes, I will do what you ask," he said as he stood to face the luminescent being.

"There is a bird," the voice began. "It is the Great Thunderbird of the sky. You must bring me a feather from its tail by the second night of the new moon. Know this: by this quest, you must not let anything keep you from fulfilling the most important purpose of your life, not anything. If you fail in this purpose, your people will live in despair for all the days of eternity. Now go and do not come back until you have succeeded," commanded the being.

The startled warrior climbed down from his high, treacherous and rocky perch, returned to his village and told his people of his vision. The next morning, the warrior set out on his quest, leaving his wife, daughter, grandson and all his people behind. He traveled for many days and nights, searching everywhere he could think of to find the Great Thunderbird. Finding the bird would be one thing. Knowing how to secure one of its tail feathers would be quite another. Legends were told of the terrifying, gigantic bird and how, in one fell swoop, it could crush even the largest of earth creatures with its powerful claws. His task was not to be undertaken with a light heart.

Growing tired and weak from wandering for so long in search of the fierce bird, the old warrior became delirious with fatigue and laid down beside a powerful river to rest. When he awoke, he was in a very strange land he had never seen before. A fine mist covered the ground and floated into the trees like spirals of smoke in a sacred dance of blessings. The warrior stood up to survey his surroundings. The trees were not like trees, exactly. At times they looked like giants with many arms and hands reaching out to grab at him.

Seeing a tall hill in the distance, he decided to make his way to the top of it for safety and to observe more of this strange place. Fighting back against the clawing limbs of the eerie trees, he ran toward the hill. Without warning, monstrous boulders came crashing down from the mountainsides along the shallow valley where he ran. The boulders barely missed him as he swiftly darted back and forth along the trail.

Suddenly, from nowhere, a terrifying wind came up like an angry tornado, lifted the warrior off his feet and swept him into the air. Higher and higher it carried him, as he screamed in fright and flailed about, trying to keep his balance. The dirt-filled wind whipped his face, making it cold and raw. As his long black hair pulled tightly away from his head, he thought it would be torn from his scalp. The pressure inside the whirlwind increased and his body felt as though it were being crushed under tons of coarse sand. He could hardly breathe, and he knew he would soon die.

Then, as rapidly as it began, the torrents of blinding wind faded away. The warrior dropped onto a spongy moss covering on top of the very hill he was running toward. Still lying on his stomach where he had fallen, the old warrior regained his senses as he looked around to see where he was. There, sitting at the very edge of the plateau with its back to him, was the largest bird he had ever seen. As it sat in quiet majesty, with its enormous wings outstretched and a magnificent tail fanned out behind it, the great bird appeared to be silently surveying its magic realm. The warrior kept still for a moment to see if it had noticed him and would make any moves to attack him.

"Surely this must be the Great Thunderbird," he thought to himself. "I must get one of its tail feathers, but how?"

Many moments passed until the warrior decided to simply sneak up behind the bird and attempt to remove one of its plumes before it took flight. He would never have another chance such as this. Sliding on his belly across the mossy ground, he wondered if the bird even knew he was there, for it never moved from its position. He was close enough now to firmly grasp a tail feather so that when the bird took flight, the feather would remove itself and be left in his hands. He quickly clasped them around the middle of one of the feathers and hung on tightly.

Instantly, in a blinding flash of light, the Great Thunderbird simply disappeared and the warrior found himself lying on his stomach, tail feather in hand, once again by the powerful river where earlier he had laid down to rest. Startled, but thrilled at his success, he set out to take the feather to the special plateau where he sat talking to the great spirits of the earth, and where he now must bestow the feather on the voice of the star.

Just as he reached the base of the rocky hill where he was to climb up to the vantage point of his spiritual place, the warrior saw his wife dangling above him. She was desperately clinging to the root of a bush growing off the side of the hill and he could hear her sobs of terror. Their small grandson was firmly attached to her back in a carrier. The daughter was on a short ledge above his wife, clinging to the side of the hill. They had been picking berries on the ledge above when part of it gave way and his wife slipped, falling to where she now clung to life by a very weak thread. She could not hang on much longer.

The warrior worked quickly as he hastily climbed the rocky ledges he knew so well. He called out to his wife to tell her he was coming and for her to hang on for a few more moments. When he reached her side, he wrapped one of his strong arms around her waist, lifting her to a place where she could get her footing and safely climb back down the hill.

Dark of night was setting in and the warrior knew he did not have much time left before the star would come to see him and demand the feather. He hastened his efforts and reached up to his daughter to guide her to safety. As he set his daughter down on a ledge of rock, her foot slipped, causing them both to lean away from the side of the hill. He reached out to grasp her with both of his hands and pull her to safety. As he did so, the feather he had been holding with such care fell from his hand and floated away on a current of air. Clutching his trembling daughter to his side, the old warrior called out in agony as he watched the feather disappear in the high trees. This was the second night of the new moon and he would not have time to search for the Great Thunderbird again. Full of sorrow, he told his wife and daughter to return to the village and tell the people of his failure.

Climbing the hill once again, the weary warrior finally reached the top, sat on the ground with his head hung low and waited for the star to appear. He did not have long to wait. The mystical star shimmered, grew immense and showered him with glaring light. No words came forth from the being, so the warrior offered the tale of his quest. He told the star how he had found the Great Thunderbird, but had lost the feather, causing him to fail in the completion of his purpose as he was instructed. He begged the star to take his life in exchange for the freedom and happiness of his people. Silence was the only answer for a moment, and the warrior sat weeping with his head bowed in shame.

After what seemed forever, the voice suddenly proclaimed in a gentle, praising tone, "You have not failed. You have made the right choice and succeeded in your most important purpose in life. Above all else, your love and commitment to your family are the ties that bind all people to their own future. You knew this in your heart and you listened."

Tears of joy and exhaustion trickled from the old warrior's eyes and moistened his folded hands. As he slowly lifted his head to gaze upon the star, his eyes met those of the Great Thunderbird surrounded by the glowing light. The majestic creature turned with its powerful wings outstretched and flew away into the night sky.

*From our family comes our life*
*to pass it 'round again.*
*This is the circle of the truth*
*that greets us in the end.*

~ ~ ~

## *THE PRINCESS AND THE BEAR*

*Once upon a smile,*
*in a land of dreams and wonder,*
*lived a fairy princess child*
*and her bear.*

*In the evening if it rained,*
*with the pounding of the thunder,*
*the princess sang a song*
*for all to hear.*

*She sang so soft and gently*
*that all the realm should know*
*they were safe from harm and loved*
*in every way.*

*Her tiny, tinkling voice*
*drifted sweetly high and low*
*as it brightly lifted spirits*
*night and day.*

*The bear, so warm and fuzzy,*
*gave the princess courage real,*
*as she comforted the souls*
*throughout the land.*

*The princess and the bear*
*had a friendship you could feel*
*and the strength of it was truly*
*something grand.*

*One day, the princess became ill*
*and the bear began to cry,*
*as he snuggled her in bed*
*and held her near.*

*When the princess fell to silence,*
*they thought that she would die,*
*but the bear would not give up,*
*he had no fear.*

*While she slept, he spoke of life*
*and all the reasons to go on, as their friendship*
*glowed throughout the days*
*and weeks.*

*He kept a careful watch beside her*
*everyday 'till each new dawn*
*and the color started coming*
*to her cheeks.*

*As the princess became stronger*
*and she spoke to all around,*
*she told them of the bear*
*and all his love.*

*And the kingdom soon returned*
*to the beauty and the sound*
*of the princess singing sweetly*
*from above.*

*Now the princess became older*
*and the bear, well he did too,*
*but their friendship lasted*
*all throughout the years.*

*And the story of their love*
*is a way for me and you*
*to know we can live through*
*any pain and tears.*

*When you come to times in life*
*that are more than you can bear,*
*remember this sweet story*
*you have read.*

*Keep courage, faith and hope*
*in your life and you will share*
*happy times*
*in all the years ahead.*

*NEVER GIVE UP*

~ ~ ~

## THE TWO OF YOU

Keep in your heart and mind,
the richness of the two of you.
Lose not your eyes for love. Seek
not in hollow places for
joys beyond the heart.
Treasure the company
of the two of you.
Remember that
double are your
sorrows, your pains
and tribulations.
Keep in mind the
hurt for the two of
you. Be as the entrance
to the door of life by
supporting that which each
of you endeavors and let not one restrain
the other. Rejoice in your double happiness,
but hide not the single joys. And remember
those who love you, who love the two of you.

~ ~ ~

# LOVE

Love doesn't take,
but that it replenishes.
Love doesn't hurt,
but that it brings joy.
Love doesn't forget,
but that it remembers all.
Love doesn't dim,
but that it grows bright again.
Love doesn't die.

~ ~ ~

# Chapter Three

## A JOURNEY THROUGH CHILDHOOD

Where do you begin with children, since they are the beginning of what we call life? Children are the celebration of our spiritual beginnings on this earth journey, before we are overpowered by our physical experiences. If you were given a balloon and told that all of the hopes and dreams for your life and future were inside that balloon, and however you cared for it determined your future, you would make sure that it never burst, sustained any damage or drifted away. A balloon is extremely delicate, fun to play with, beautiful to see and helpless as to its fate. So are children. Nurture and help children to celebrate life and you will be celebrating the spiritual child within yourself.

Ahhhhhhhhhhhhhhh . . .
life without children;
No mess
No noise
No laundry
No dishes
No cooking
No love
No caring
No sharing
No laughter
. . . No life.

## THE FOREVER CHILD

The newborn child,
with its tiny grasp,
holds all the world
in its hand.

The infant child,
with eyes so clear,
sees all of life
as grand.

The toddler child
learns to cry
for reasons
new to him.

The pre-school child
shows creative growth
and builds things
on a whim.

The grade school child
finds in life
new ways to speak
her mind.

The teenage child
learns lessons
which sometimes
are unkind.

The high school child
explores his mind
and his image
of himself.

The college child
makes life's designs
from her ideas
of life's "wealth".

The adult child
carries out
all the lessons
he has learned.

The aged child
remembers back
on the seasons that
have turned.

Please give your child
a special life
filled with love
and caring true.

For when you're old
the child in you
will want to have
them too.

~ ~ ~

## COME PLAY IN THE SANDBOX

Come play in the sandbox
and you will see
the world of the child
in you and me.

A castle, a dragon
and animals too,
in a mountain of sand,
there's so much to do.

A butterfly, beetles
and fairies with wings.
Can you imagine
so many things?

Let's celebrate life
and the wonders to see.
Come play in the sandbox
with my friends and me.

~ ~ ~

## CHILDISH THOUGHTS ...

- Once a parent, always a parent, but never an owner of their soul.

- Parents of critically ill children become the ambassadors of their survival.

- The teenage years are a delicate balance between the desire for freedom, and the fear of being let go.

- Children live life in such a simple way. Why is it that the most complex thing for adults to achieve is simplicity?

- Children are a gift for the future, but too often they are victims of the past. If you truly want to control your future, let go of your own past and be loving and kind to children.

~ ~ ~

## CHILD OF MINE

I saw my child today
and knew I had talked with God.
How perfect a form could be,
by the pain of life untrod.

The innocence I saw
gave me to remember mine.
With freshness of time not passed,
like new fruit laced upon the vine.

Without words, I saw the love
and trust in those who share,
to teach and guide with gentleness,
the lessons of life to bear.

My child is a gift to me,
this I do truly know,
to teach me the emotion of love,
no matter the mind I show.

In the reaches of my heart and soul,
my gratitude is deep
to a universe which knows
of the tears that I did weep.

If never I had been blessed
with this child now close to me,
how could I learn so much of life
through the eyes that I now see?

This tiny hand and tender face,
so trusting, sweet and pure,
a trembling chin and faltering limbs,
like a fawn; fragile and unsure.

Thank you God of the universe
for sharing your miracle with me.
I shall honor your trust
and allow this soul to be whole and free.

Free from the burden of lack, not of things,
but of friendship and caring love,
to give of myself and not shear the wings
of this gentle little dove.

The winds of change will carry
my child away too soon,
these moments of newness to recall
like the rays of each new moon.

Like a garden planted to bloom forever,
each spring to view the spray,
these moments and those to come,
in my heart eternally stay.

A part of life, a part of me
to carry the seeds of time.
Life is good and I see the love
in this beautiful child of mine.

~ ~ ~

## POPCORN AND PICKLES

Popcorn and pickles,
shoelace and nickels,
a lion is on the phone!

Pogo sticks and tree stumps,
big bugs and blue bumps,
a fish is burying a bone!

Row boats and mud pies,
pink frogs and shoe flies,
help, a bee is throwing clay!

Popsicles and pine cones,
tall twigs and square stones,
now a cow has come to play.

Light bulbs and licorice,
green cats and fuzzy fish,
chickens aren't supposed to fly!

Peacocks without their tails,
rocking chairs and ringing bells,
a sloth is running by!

Puff balls and jelly beans,
tall mice and silly jeans,
and now a sleeping hare!

An ostrich with purple stuff,
a bat with striped fluff,
now how did that get there?

String balls and pencil ends,
hair clips and chairs that bend,
I think I'm going nuts!

Coconuts with hairy legs,
bed posts and pirate pegs,
there's hippos in those huts!

Over there is a parakeet,
with flippers on both its feet,
and a mouse is playing on a drum!

Believe me, if I had known
what Martha had in her home,

I never would have come! ! !

~ ~ ~

~ ❖ ~

## FOX AND MOUSE

On a wonderfully stormy day, as the wind whistled its warning of a cool rain to come, a fox was busy sniffing through the grass when suddenly, he came upon a mouse. Now, being quite hungry, the fox thought to eat the mouse, and being very frightened, the mouse thought to trick the fox.

With his mouth wide open in readiness to gulp down the tiny creature, the fox lunged toward it. "Wait," shouted the mouse. "Do you not like yourself?"

The fox stopped instantly and replied, "Of course I like myself. I am beautiful and clever."

"But not clever enough to know that if you eat me, you will do harm to yourself," the mouse replied cautiously.

"How can that possibly be?" snapped the fox. "I am a fox and you are a mouse. I am much larger than you, and we are not even the same color. I have a beautiful coat of red fur and you are very dull and grey. You are talking nonsense and I am going to eat you right now." The fox reopened his jaws and started for the mouse.

"Suit yourself," squeaked the mouse. "You will never know the answer if I am dead and inside of you."

Becoming quite annoyed, but curious at this point, the fox stopped again and growled, "Oh, all right, tell me what you have to say and then I will eat you."

"I cannot just tell you," said the mouse with a sigh of relief. "It is far more important than that. Come with me to the pond and you will see what I mean."

The two forest neighbors traveled a great distance through the thick woods and lush green underbrush on their way to the pond. Along the way, they stopped to eat berries, nuts and insects, and lick the dew from the blades of sweet grass. Occasionally, they stopped to rest by a hollowed out tree root, or a plump log covered with fuzzy, warm moss. Suddenly, the sky filled with soft, grey clouds and a light spring rain gently sprinkled the earth with miniature drops of moisture.

As the fox and mouse meandered along the path to the pond, they talked to each other about their lives. The mouse told the fox about her family and her plans for the future. She talked of how much she loved playing in the meadow and running about in the forest. The fox laughed and agreed that life was indeed wonderful and he too enjoyed these very same things. It was truly amazing how much they did have in common.

After a while, they arrived at the pond and the mouse ran to the edge to look out over the water. She sighed a big sigh as she turned back to the fox and said, "I am so sorry. I cannot show you what I wanted. Because the rain is making too many ripples on the surface of the pond, we will not be able to see our reflections."

The fox looked thoughtfully at the little mouse and calmly replied, "Well, I am really too full from eating all those berries and nuts anyway, so I will just have to let you go today." The mouse smiled her tiny smile and went on her way.

*Very often we will find*
*the differences in others,*
*are simply shadowed by the time*
*we take to know our brothers.*

~ ~ ~

## CHORE WARS!

It's always time
to do the chores,
make the beds
and sweep the floors,
fold the clothes
and clean the sink.
Don't you agree,
chores really stink!

Chores are boring
and really dumb.
I'm at the age
when I need fun.
I'm just a kid,
I need to play.
I can't do chores
night and day.

My hands are wrinkled
my skin is "pruned."
My social life,
is totally ruined.
You can't be serious
about doing all this.
Just think of all
the fun I'll miss.

My friends will never
call me again.
My entire life
is going to end.
They won't know
who I am anymore,
if you keep me doing
chore after chore.

Please let me make
just one more call,
and I promise
I will finish it all.
I'm sure no one
will remember my name,
because I'm late
for the afternoon game.

How can it be time
again so soon?
I just did all this
on the last full moon.
I picked up the floor,
even under my bed.
Well, actually I pushed
stuff under instead.

I really can't take this
for too much longer.
You're lucky I'm young
and so much stronger.
I must have been doing this
for hours and hours.
I even took the hair balls
out of the shower.

I hung up my clothes,
well, yes the dirty ones too,
but who knows the difference,
I sure haven't a clue!
I made my bed, well, yes,
with unclean sheets,
but they'll get dirty again
from the gunk on my feet.

Before I'm done,
I'll be wrinkled and old,
and have all gray hair.
Can't this stuff just be sold?
Did I hear you say,
it's only been thirty?
You can't mean minutes,
this place was so dirty.

What's that you say,
I'm almost done?
Wait a minute,
I was having fun.
For a while there,
I actually felt great,
doing all the stuff
I usually hate.

Well, thank you,
it does look nice.
I guess half an hour
is a fair price,
for a clean room
and clear path to my bed.
Chores aren't as boring
as everyone said.

Thanks mom and dad,
I love you too,
and please let me know
what else I can do.
Well, let's save it
for another day.
I'll just change my clothes
and be on my way.

~ ~ ~

## THE FIRST SPRING OF YOUNG ADULTS

The world is yours,
to love or hate,
to give or take,
forever.

Remember you were a child
when you first started in this world,
and you will be old one day too.
Respect them both.

Seek out your strengths
and forgive your weaknesses.
Know you are the future,
for everyone.

It is an awesome responsibility,
an infinite opportunity,
an open door,
for you.

Help heal the earth.
It gives you life.
It is your home
and reflects your care.

Share only the love and encouragement
you have been given.
Let go of the anger
You do not need it.

Start fresh from this moment on.
It is a new page in a great book
about you,
written by you.

Be proud of your endeavors.
They reflect who you are
and what you want
your own life to be.

Partake of celebrations
with a full heart
and a clear mind,
they will be your stimulus.

When you are tired, rest.
No one achieved greatness
in one day,
or one hour.

This is the first spring
of your adult life,
of your future,
forever.

You are magnificent youth!
Go in peace and be kind
to each other,
always.

~ ~ ~

## TICKLED PINK

A fairy is a tiny soul,
with special magic powers.
They tiptoe and they twinkle,
as they giggle through all hours.

You say you've never seen one?
Well, I tell you that's not true.
There are many, many times in life
when fairies visit you.

There is a very special one
who is busier than the rest.
She flits and floats throughout the world,
giving everyone her best.

She knows just when to show herself
and when to hide away.
She brings her joy to all of life
and someone special everyday.

If someone's gone and then returns,
she's there to spark the glee,
inspiring people's shouts of joy
over someone that they see.

On birthday celebration days
she never stops to rest.
She twirls and twinkles very bright,
pleasing every guest.

When brand new pets arrive at home
and the family gathers 'round,
she's there to make you happy
with the new friend you have found.

If you see your grandparents
and visit for a while,
she's there when grandpa makes you laugh
and when grandma makes you smile.

When your best friend comes to play
and spend some time with you,
she's there to make you laugh and sing,
having fun in all you do.

She's truly been around you
more often than you think.
Every time you're happy, she's there
and her name is Tickled Pink.

Now that you know she's always there
for you to call to you,
just close your eyes and imagine her,
she'll arrive in a wink or two.

Remember when you're feeling sad
and you need to laugh and smile,
Tickled Pink will be with you,
twinkling all the while.

~ ~ ~

## OUR CHILDREN . . .

See life in a simple way, not right or wrong,
but by what they are accustomed to.
They are like tiny, delicate seeds.
Nurturing and patient love
are what help them grow healthy.

When they are babies they cry,
only because they cannot speak words yet.
If you are angry or impatient with them,
they cry out of fear and anxiety.
Hold them, cradle them, touch them
only with the greatest of respect.

If you were treated with disrespect
when you were young, don't repeat the pattern.
It will only hurt them as much as it hurt you.
Be strong enough to be different
from the adults in your childhood.

When they are toddlers, they speak the words
they have heard others speak.
Talk to them gently, in earnest.
If they play with something they cannot have,
don't grab it away from them
and leave them empty-handed.
Trade it for something they can have.
Grabbing only startles them
and makes them fearful,
and soon they learn to grab things
away from others.

When they are adolescents, they are emotional,
because they are trying out their emotions,
like when they are learning to ride a bike.

At first they are awkward and uncomfortable
with the new emotions they experience.
If they are allowed to feel these emotions
while maintaining respect for those around
them
and are gently guided through them
without fear,
they will keep the good emotions
and let the bad ones go.

Don't make fun of them.
Remember, you were their age once
and you had the same feelings.
If you were made fun of when you were young,
have the courage to be different, and loving.
Give them the respect that you did not have.
How you treat your children
when they are young,
is how they will treat you
when you are old.

Teenagers are strong-willed and independent,
not because they don't love you,
but because they are learning how to relate to,
or be in love with their peers.
Their friends are all changing,
and going in different directions.

The groups of kids they were close to
in their adolescent years are all changing too;
changing homes, parents, friends, values,
experiences, and experiments.

They watch with fear and anxiety
as they see some of the good friends
they were once close to
change for the worse, become unhappy
and frustrated.
These changes frighten them.

They see their own bodies changing.
Their moods become more intense,
as they cry and scream a lot.
Don't take it personally.
Let them have their feelings
with respect toward you and others,
but let them feel without fear.

If they tell you they hate you
when you make them do chores,
or clean their room,
acknowledge their feelings and tell them
you are sure that is how they feel right now,
but they still have to do as they were asked.
They don't really hate you,
just the duty of cleaning their room.

Kids get bored easily,
mostly when there are no adults around
who will spend time with them
doing things kids like to do.
Even if you think an activity is silly,
don't say so, just do it with them.
It tells them they are important
and that they make good choices.

Kids collect little things, like scraps of paper,
dead flowers, stacks of pictures of their friends,
rocks, pieces of plastic, or maybe a pop tab
that one of their friends gave them
in a tender, humorous moment.

Don't throw away their memories.
When they have outgrown them,
they will throw them away on their own,
or pack them away
for tomorrow's memories.

Their music is often loud
and can even be offensive.
Patiently let them know the words or sounds
can be offensive to some,
but let them decide for themselves
to stop listening to it, or not.
You cannot be inside their head,
and you don't need to be.
Have faith that you are inside their hearts.

Be a good example,
but don't try to make your children
be just like you, or force them to do the things
you wish you could have done
when you were their age.
They have their own personalities and ideas.
Enjoy and celebrate the variety
of having individuals in your family.

Listen to your children talk, even if you think
what they are saying is silly or boring.
Don't make them feel silly for talking to you,
or they will stop talking to you altogether.
None of us is brilliant or interesting all the
time.
Laugh at their jokes and humor,
even if you have heard it all before.

Let your children find their own level
of educational performance.
If they are having trouble,
ask them why they think it is happening.
Ask them what they would do
to change it if they could.

Let them choose healthy activities
that appeal to them.
Simply tell them that whatever they choose,
they must commit to one year of attending
all the practices, performances, or whatever
is required for that particular activity.

At the end of that year,
if they don't want to do the same thing again,
they can decide at the beginning
of the next year.
You'll be surprised how often
they'll choose to do it again.
Patiently and earnestly help them be
at all the places they need to be
to fulfill and complete this commitment.

Attend as many of their special events
as you possibly can.
It tells them you are proud of them,
and that you like what they are doing.
Most of all, be there for them as teammates,
as parents, as friends.
Remember, you brought them into the world
and they do not live with you for very long
before they are out on their own.

Relive your childhood through their eyes,
by watching them grow up with you.
Before you worry about giving them
all the material things in life,
give them the mental health
to enjoy everything.
No matter how much they, or you acquire,
if they are unhappy inside,
no material things will bring them peace.

Hug, protect, defend and admire your children.
Don't use the phrase,
"When you get out into the real world."
Respect the reality of their world.
It is just as real as yours.
Show them you are human,
and that you can cry,
laugh and play.
Be their guardian and true friend,
and most of all remember . . .

*Children imitate,*
*just as you did.*

~ ~ ~

## THE ILLEGITIMATE CHILD

If God were cold and angry,
he would surely turn away
from the child born of "sin"
and not of "holy clay."

But there is no child born
who has no right to be,
for God is truly part
of the life in all we see.

To make a child's birth
an "illegal" part of life,
is to cause a human pain
from double-sided knife.

It's not just the woman's deed
which made the life that she will bear.
Someday the man must face
his child standing there.

If a man declines to claim
all the children he begets,
how can he face his God
without facing his regrets?

There's no such thing as "legal,"
for the truth will not be guiled,
and the world cannot proclaim
there's even one illegitimate child.

~ ~ ~

# BEFORE

**Before there was hate,
before there was war,
before there was fear of each other,
there were children,
and we taught them to hate,
we taught them to war,
we taught them to fear each other,
and teach their children.
Children are a gift to adults,
to learn from, to teach a better way
than the way before, that didn't work,
to feel a deeper love than the love before,
that was hidden,
to see through the children's eyes,
a world which not yet knows of them,
to feel through their emotions,
a fresh, unstrained eagerness to learn.
Teach them love, kindness,
empathy and courage.
Teach them to have convictions
in their own beliefs
and teach them that today
their efforts will bring about
a better tomorrow.**

~ ~ ~

## PIGGLE PIGGLE MUCK MUCK

Piggle Piggle Muck Muck
loved to run and play.
He tumbled and he rumbled,
in the mud and crumpled hay.

He ran around the barnyard
playing everywhere he could.
He even stuck his snout
in the stack of cherry wood.

Piggle loved his mud
more than anything on earth.
He was very sad without it
and had been that way since birth.

Now, Grey Granny Goose
planned a party in the barn.
She invited all the animals
who lived there on the farm.

For days before the party
everyone got clean,
except for Piggle Piggle Muck Muck.
He created quite a scene.

He refused to take a bath
or wash between his toes.
He liked the mud he played in,
even in his nose!

"If you are coming to my party,
you better clean up good,"
said Grey Granny Goose,
though she thought he never would.

The party day arrived
and everyone was ready,
except Piggle Piggle Muck Muck.
He was holding steady.

Well, not one soul allowed him
to come into the barn.
They told him he was dirty
and it would not do him harm,

to take a bath and clean up
so he could play with all the rest.
They said that it would do him good,
to dress up in his best.

So, Piggle took a shower
and cleaned up in the stall.
Everyone had lots of fun,
and Piggle had a ball.

~ ~ ~

~ ❖ ~

## THE WIZ THAT WASN'T

Wizards are very special souls who are supposed to use their magic to help others solve their problems. Whimzy the Wizard did not use his magic for anything but silliness and play. Now, being silly and playing are very important things to do, but not all of the time. Whimzy knew he could be a great wizard, but he only wanted to play foolish tricks on others.

One day, Mrs. Bimble Bee flew past Whimzy on her way to a Gumberry Tree grove and she bumped right into the wizard.

"Excuse me Whimzy. I didn't see you standing there. I'm very sorry that I bumped into you," buzzed Mrs. Bee. "I'm on my way to see the Gumberry Trees open their beautiful blossoms today. I just love to smell those pretty flowers and taste that sweet pollen inside."

"Well, then let me help you," giggled Whimzy as he waved his magic wand and changed the bee into a gumberry blossom with wings.

"Help," yelled the bee, "Change me back you silly wizard! I don't want to be a blossom. I just want to smell them and collect the pollen for food."

Whimzy laughed so hard that he fell down.

"You change me back right now. This is not funny at all," shouted Mrs. Bee.

"Oh, all right, but you're no fun," said Whimzy as he stood up and waved his wand over the bee.

Mrs. Bee turned back into a bee and flew away. No sooner had she disappeared than a large Rooker's Rat came scurrying out of the bushes and bumped right into Whimzy's foot.

"Excuse me, Mr. Wizard. I didn't see you standing there. I'm sorry that I bumped into you," squeaked Mr. Rat. "I'm on my way to the Waving Wheat Fields. The grain will be falling to the ground today and there will be lots to eat."

"Well, then let me help you," said Whimzy as he giggled once again, waved his magic wand over the rat and turned him into a stalk of wheat with a long tail.

"Help," yelled the rat, "Change me back you silly wizard. This is not funny at all. I don't want to be a stalk of wheat. I just want to gather the crunchy seeds and eat them."

Whimzy laughed so hard, his hat fell off of his head and he sat down on the ground to keep from falling over again.

"Change me back right now!" shouted Mr. Rat.

"Oh, all right, but you're no fun," said Whimzy as he waved his wand over the rat once more.

Mr. Rat turned back into a rat and ran away.

Suddenly, a giant Bugle Bull Frog hopped from the pond, right into the wizard's lap. The startled wizard jumped up and as he did so, his magic wand flew from his hand through the air and landed on top of the water in the middle of the pond. Whimzy could not swim, or use his magic because he did not have his wand.

"Now, that is a funny sight indeed," croaked Mr. Frog as he laughed and laughed.

"That isn't the least bit funny," shouted Whimzy. "I can't do my magic without my wand. You have to go out there and get it for me right now."

"I don't have to do anything," laughed the frog as he started to hop away. "You can't even turn me into something else because you don't have your magic wand, so I'm leaving."

The Bugle Bull Frog hopped into the tall reeds next to the pond and left the wizard all alone, without his wand. Whimzy the Wizard was not laughing anymore. How was he ever going to get his magic wand back? At that moment, the Rooker's Rat came scampering back from the wheat fields and ran past Whimzy.

"Oh dear Mr. Rat," cried Whimzy, "Please go out into the pond and help me get my wand back. I must have it."

"I don't like the water," said Mr. Rat, "but I will go and find Mrs. Bee if you promise never to play tricks on us again."

“Oh, I promise from now on I will only use my magic to help others,” said the wizard.

Mr. Rat saw that Whimzy was very earnest in his promise so he ran off to find Mrs. Bee. They soon returned to the pond and Mrs. Bee flew out over the water and picked up the floating magic wand. She brought it over to Whimzy and he thanked her for her help.

*When you take a joke too far,*
*that hurts others in the end,*
*you take away from who you are,*
*and you can lose a friend.*

~ ~ ~

# I CHOSE YOU

I adopted a child today,
because I needed to share my love
        and this child needed me.
        I opened up my heart and home
to this tiny human soul,
a parent at last to be.

        No matter that I did not birth
        this precious little child,
I am the one who loves and cares.
This child, now my child,
        will be forever a part of my life,
        which I will always share.

Please know, little one,
you are important and loved.
        You are here on earth to live.
        I will honor and cherish you always.
Your new life, now with me,
will be the best that I can give.

        Whatever the reason could be
        for you to come into my life
as an adopted child today,
I now enfold you in my arms,
        take you into my heart and soul
        where you will forever and ever stay.

~ ~ ~

## THE SCENT OF PREY

The gudgeon of another day,
will leave the trace and scent of prey,
for predators to know and smell,
to capture and deliver hell.

Born to earth to learn of fear,
longing for the end to near,
to give the soul its freedom soon,
to dance about the sun and moon.

The human beast knows all too well,
to teach the fear and cast the spell,
that breaks the spirit's will to live,
and commands the soul to not forgive.

The physical gains a steady lead,
and leaves the broken soul to bleed,
from wounds inflicted there from birth,
to show the scars of life on earth.

A rabbit or a mouse could be,
so tiny, yet so plain to see.
The carnivore is never far,
inflicting wounds that leave the scar.

The lessons learned, some too late,
to shield the soul from rage and hate,
yet coping comes once again,
in hopes the pain and tears will end.

Survival is the strongest link,
that instructs the mind on how to think,
and teaches the child a victim play,
wretched with the scent of prey.

~ ~ ~

## YOU'VE GOT IT!

You're on that shaky foot again,
the one that feels so weak.
You've got that lumpy throat again,
the one that cannot speak.
You've got that quivering hand again,
the one that cannot grasp, but
you've got that stubborn will again,
the one that always lasts !

~ ~ ~

~ ❖ ~

## THE TREASURE HUNT

In a quiet meadow surrounded by majestic trees and billowing bushes, two children played make-believe. Towering over the meadow, stood a rugged, and very magic mountain. A kingdom resting at the top of this mountain was inhabited by only the wisest of souls and no one else knew exactly how to get there. The only visible access was a steep, treacherous road from which many people simply disappeared while trying to navigate its dangerous terrain.

On this warm, fall day, a young girl and boy were in the meadow pretending to be the rulers of this mystical, mountain kingdom. They draped themselves in shawls woven from the tall grasses, and created noble crowns from wreaths of sorrel leaves and daisies. A large boulder became their throne, holding them high above the ground so they could survey the entire meadow. From this regal perch, they pledged their unending loyalty to their royal subjects; the meadow's animal life. Birds chirped as if in approval of these two small humans who would be their protectors. Bees hummed and a woodpecker kept a steady beat, filling the entire meadow with a symphony of living sounds, uninterrupted and hypnotic in its rhythm.

The children were mesmerized as they stood in peaceful anticipation of the royal coronation when their imaginary court server would place the official crowns upon their heads. As they held hands, they closed their eyes to imagine themselves on the mountain top.

No sooner had they closed their eyes, then they were standing in front of the real king and queen inside the great hall of the magic kingdom. Startled, but excited by what had just happened to them, they listened intently as the queen spoke to them in a loving, but firm voice, "By your youthful innocence and imagination you have discovered the secret to entering our world, but you must earn the right to stay."

The king began to tell them of the task they were to complete in order to pass a strange test; one that no one had been successful at for a long time. The children were handed a small egg and given these instructions:

"Take this egg and go into the deep forest. You must not return to us until you have found the secret to life. You see around you in this great hall many useless things that others brought back to us and so failed the test. If you do not succeed in this task, you will be banished to the haze of ignorance, never to be seen again," stated the king.

The anxious children closed their eyes to imagine being in the woods and immediately found themselves deep in the darkest reaches of the forest. They did not know where they were or how to find their way out. They could close their eyes and imagine themselves out of the forest, but they would then have failed the test and they knew the king and queen would summon them to the kingdom by their own royal thoughts. They would have to face their punishment anyway, so they simply accepted their fate and started on their adventure. Tucking the fragile egg into her sash, the girl decided they could eat it later if they were not able to find any other food, and they began their search for this most peculiar and difficult request.

Looking under every rock, log and leaf, searching every cave, hollow tree and burrow, climbing tall trees, sifting through acres of soil, and examining every possible item they came across, the children pursued their task with the most heartfelt effort. Feeling certain that the precious stones and glittering objects they found were not the answer, they searched and searched for three days, but produced nothing they could believe was the secret to life.

They ate berries and nuts when they could find them, but now they were hungry and lost. Suddenly, the girl remembered the egg hidden in her sash and as she reached for it, her sash began to wriggle. A small peeping noise came from inside the gentle folds of cloth. The egg had hatched!

Exasperated and frightened, the boy stared at the baby bird, "We have not done as we were asked and if we stay here longer we will all die anyway. We must take the bird back to the kingdom so it can live, and we will face our punishment together."

They agreed and then imagined themselves in the great hall, standing before the royal couple.

"We have returned to bring you this sweet

baby bird that hatched from the egg you sent with us," offered the young girl as she lifted it up to the queen.

"We are sorry we were not able to find anything that we thought could possibly be the secret to life," lamented the boy. "We will accept our punishment."

Receiving the tiny bird, and holding it up for all to see, the queen replied, "You have done well children. You did not settle for some false and foolish treasure simply to appease us. You have brought us the secret to life: life itself. Welcome to our world. You will learn much here."

*The boundless treasures in this life,*
*which are the grandest find,*
*are the pearls of wisdom, truth and love,*
*within the human mind.*

~ ~ ~

## WHEN RAINBOWS CRY

Rainbows glow with bright tomorrows
and promises of sun.
People stop to catch the colors,
a new day has begun.

Rainbows laugh and dance with wonder
at birds who flutter near.
Lightly, moisture fills the senses,
quieting all fear.

Rainbows sing as clouds give way
to warmth and softer air.
The music ripples o'er hills and valleys,
the world has not a care.

'Till a voice cries out in timeless pain,
"A child has come to die."
The agony brings tears of sadness,
and that's when rainbows cry.

~ ~ ~

## WHAT OH WHAT OH WHAT DID YOU SAY?

Ba ba bing bong boo ba bay.
Da da ding dong doo da day.

Fa fa fing fong foo fa fay.
Ga ga ging gong goo ga gay.

Ha ha hing hong hoo ha hay.
Ka ka king kong koo ka kay.

La la ling long loo la lay.
Ma ma ming mong moo ma may.

Na na ning nong noo na nay.
Pa pa ping pong poo pa pay.

Ra ra ring rong roo ra ray.
Sa sa sing song soo sa say.

Ta ta ting tong too ta tay.
Va va ving vong voo va vay.

Wa wa wing wong woo wa way.
Ya ya ying yong yoo ya yay.

Za za zing zong zoo za zay.

Now that you know the words to say,
please tell the Martian he can stay!!

~ ~ ~

## MY FRIEND, MY TEACHER, MY CHILD

You've become a woman now
and truly my best friend.
You've spent your life showing me
how to love and how to mend
the pain of all that we've been through,
the tears we both have shed.
I cherish every hug and kiss
and wise words you have said.

I'm so proud of all that you have done
in your few short years of life.
You've kept your spirit up so high
through all your grief and strife.
You've always known the way to go
when we reached a bumpy road,
and God knows, my grown up woman child,
you've carried a heavy load.

So thank you, daughter, I love you so
and I cherish all the fun.
You've shown me how to part the clouds
and find the hiding sun.
As you go forward in this life,
please know I'll always care.
I'll be with you forever, child,
through the lifetimes that we share.

~ ~ ~

## THE FUTURE

If you want to know the future
of the world where we now live,
if you want to know how people
will learn to take or give,
if you want to know if life
will be angry, kind or mild,
just watch the way we teach
the present to a child.

~ ~ ~

## ABOUT THE AUTHOR

A. Marie B. is a native of Washington State and a true survivor who has learned to celebrate her life's journey. She is a woman of courage and strength, who for over thirty years of her life, has recorded her observations and stories about life.

Some of her adventures came from her childhood in foster homes, being widowed at age twenty six, and spending over a dozen years dealing with her daughter's life threatening bone marrow illness.

A. Marie B. believes that, although we are different races of people with different cultures, we share one spirit in having this human experience together.

**HANG IN THERE !**

# INDEX

# INDEX

# INDEX

## INDEX